MW01681443

# Secrets in the Snowdrops

*A Betty Benino Mystery, book 3*

JANET FIX

***Secrets in the Snowflakes***
***A Betty Benino Mystery, Book 3***

Copyright © 2026 Janet Fix
All Rights Reserved

No part of this book may be reproduced, stored in a retrieval system, or transmitted in any form or by any means—electronic, mechanical, photocopying, recording, or otherwise—without prior written permission of the publisher, except for brief quotations used in reviews or permitted by copyright law.

This is a work of fiction. Names, characters, places, and events are either the product of the author's imagination or used in a fictional manner. Any resemblance to actual persons, living or deceased, is purely coincidental.

First edition 2026
Published in Canton, GA, USA by *thewordverve*
**(www.thewordverve.com)**

eBook ISBN: 978-1-956856-89-7
Paperback ISBN: 978-1-956856-90-3

*Cover and interior design by Robin Krauss*
*www.bookformatters.com*
*eBook formatting by thewordverve*

# Prologue

It's been just over a year since we brought little Lucas into the world—twelve months of sleepless nights, sticky kisses, and an endless supply of laundry. We've been happily hunkered down in Chickadee Cove since then, and while we haven't made too many trips up to Bluejay Ridge, Mom has more than made up for that by coming down to visit. A lot.

And I mean a *lot.*

She calls it *helping*. I call it *loving interference*. I love her, of course I do—but if I ever see her reorganizing my pantry again, I might lose my mind.

"Who doesn't alphabetize their spices?" she'd asked, all motherly innocence.

"Normal people," I'd replied

Still, Lucas lights up every time he sees her. She's his world—and that of Emma and Jacob's too. Her grandchildren are her everything, and they know it well and good. And if Lucas grows up with a curious glimmer in his eye and a flair for the dramatic, we'll all know where that came from.

Right now, Mom's got her hands full with a historical society fundraiser. They've really put a lot of faith in her creative writing skills and ability to rally a group of worker bees when needed. And . . . she's up there, and not down here.

Though I'll be missing her soon enough.

It's our thing.

*— Genevieve Benino Marshall*

# Chapter One

"What are you up to, you little nut?" I mused, peering out the front window of my cottage home. Nutty the squirrel was particularly manic today, bounding from one side of the yard to the other with no obvious results.

As if on cue, Nutty stopped and stared back at me, his nose wriggling.

"Oh, fine." I set down my mug filled with lemon-ginger tea. It was not my favorite brew, but it was in my favorite mug—designed by my granddaughter, Emma—a replica of Nutty holding a video game controller.

More than a year had passed since my family visited the cottage for the holidays, and with good reason. My daughter, Genevieve, had blessed us all with another baby boy, who turned one last month. Long trips were not on their bingo card as a result, so I made it a point to visit them in Coastal South Georgia as often as possible this past year. But I always looked forward to coming home to the mountains. To my cozy cottage. To my friends.

I grabbed a handful of peanuts that I kept at the ready for Nutty, who'd become like a family pet. Or maybe this was a different squirrel but a lookalike, a new generation. I didn't know how the squirrel community worked.

Opening the front door, I tossed the peanuts onto the porch. A sharp breeze snuck inside, blowing my hair back, and I gasped from nature's chilly kiss.

"Go find a hole to snuggle into, Nutty Boy," I said, then closed the door against the wind. Back at the window, I saw him scurrying up the steps to collect his treats. "And stay out of the tulips." I'd planted countless bulbs a few months back in preparation for a burst of new season color. Tulips, daffodils, crocuses . . . and snowdrops, a winter favorite of mine. Those brave little snowdrops already peeked through the brittle mulch by my front walkway . . . like white whispers of spring.

I lived in a cottage community called Lake Pointe, tucked within the gorgeous lakeside town of Bluejay Ridge, and the whole place was dotted with lingering patches of ice and snow.

Springtime couldn't come soon enough. This past winter had been particularly brutal for the area with clusters of days with snow and dangerous icy conditions. I'd come to realize country mountainfolk were used to it. I, on the other hand, was not.

My home smelled of rejuvenating rosemary. I boiled fresh sprigs in a pot on the stove every other day or so, fresh from the herb tray in my kitchen window. I took my warm mug of tea and folded into the couch, my knees tucked beneath me. On the coffee table was a prime rib sandwich from O'Malley's. I was a waitress at the pub now, though very part-time, typically working the early crowd. I enjoyed the camaraderie *and* the extra cash, which I spent heedlessly on my grandchewies and garden goodies for the cottage.

I nibbled on the sandwich and picked up the seed catalog from the coffee table, though I'd buy most all my supplies from Serenity Garden Center. I was probably one of their best customers; and Tootie was doing a downright fabulous job bringing in the latest products and the very best of seeds and plants. I flipped through a few pages, and thinking of a few new ideas, I grabbed my folio from the purse at my feet and jotted them down in my growing list called *This Year's Spring Garden.*

When I moved north across Georgia to Bluejay Ridge, I was a widowed screenwriter looking for a fresh start. Now I was *someone* in town, not just the woman who'd stumbled upon a murdered accountant on one of her first days in town. Not just the woman who kept sticking her nose into the investigation—stirring the pot, as they say. Gradually dipping my toe into new adventures, I had become a treasured friend, a coworker, a community volunteer, and a garden enthusiast. The O'Malley's shifts. Helping at Millie's Bakery when needed. Volunteering at the historical society, a place where stories lived.

I also engaged in some fun activities that I'd never previously considered. Learning to drive and dock a boat on Lake Bluejay. Diving under the water and actually getting my hair wet—in front of everyone and not caring a whit. Meeting up with Hank Whitfield for cocktails every third Thursday. Shopping and gossiping with my two new besties, Trudy and Jolene.

People waved when I walked past. Some stopped to chat and toss some news around.

I was no longer the outsider. I was Betty Tater Benino, a Bluejay Ridge long-termer.

I took a sip, and the warmth spread through me. Truth was, I longed for something more. A flyer for the Bluejay Ridge Historical Society's upcoming fundraiser peeked out from under my seed catalog, but even that felt more like busywork than adventure.

Had my life become too pleasant? Too perfect? Was that a thing?

But that was what I'd been looking for.

Right?

The moments passed as I stared at the wall. No plans for the entire rest of the day.

Thankfully, Trudy called.

# Chapter Two

"She's always been the quiet type," Trudy said, flipping the blinker as they turned onto Chestnut Drive. "But lately? I don't know, she sounded more ... twitchy, I guess is the word."

"Miss Virginia is twitchy?" I asked, dubious.

"Mm-hmm." Trudy adjusted her sunglasses. "Said she had something important for the historical society—sounded like a donation, the way she put it. Maybe not specifically for the fundraiser, but close enough. Between you and me, she doesn't want to give anything up without a proper song and dance. With Virginia, everything's a performance."

I could appreciate that, but it hardly seemed accurate. My understanding was the woman was more of a recluse than any kind of drama queen. "I wonder why she called you instead of Ralph or one of us volunteers, even." Ralph Jenkins was the president of the Bluejay Ridge Historical Society.

"She did call him. He's recovering from the flu, and someone else—can't remember who—is taking over his duties. So, Virginia called me and told me to bring *you* here to the house. I probably know her better than most people. Her family and mine grew up together up in these parts, though most of us are dead as rocks or close to it."

"Trudy Carter! Don't say things like that." But I nudged her arm, chuckling, anyway. She pretended to swerve back and forth on the road. I couldn't hold back a squeak of alarm. "Hey, now. Don't push it!"

Trudy cackled, a familiar gravelly sound. "You are one of my favorite people, Tater. Always good for a laugh." Tater was my maiden name, Southern as fried okra, and every once in a while, the townsfolk thought it funny to remind me of it. "Point is, Virginia and I have known each other for gads of ages. Neither of us have siblings, and I'm the only one with a kid. Long live the Carter name."

"I'll toast to that," I said. "We've certainly had some wonderful donations for the fundraiser so far. I'm curious about whatever Miss Virginia has in store for us."

"Might be a block of wood, for all we know," Trudy said. "Don't get your panties twisted just yet."

The historical society was having a fundraiser to fix what needed fixing—roof, wiring, climate control—and to keep the town's history from literally falling apart. It had become quite the event, with donations coming in at a steady clip. The whole town—roughly seven thousand residents, plus a healthy dose of tourists—seemed eager to turn out and celebrate Bluejay Ridge's past, its notable figures, and its long-kept artifacts.

I'd learned so much since I started volunteering there; in fact, it had become one of the most fulfilling things I'd done in a long while. My biggest responsibility was writing marketing materials and short scripts about the town's heritage, and more than once I caught myself drifting into fiction land. Storytelling was in my blood, I supposed. I kept those little side pieces tucked into my folio, maybe to revisit one day—another screenplay, or even a book.

*But not today.*

"Here we are," Trudy said.

The old Victorian at 118 Chestnut came into view in the flat winter afternoon: faded blue paint, white trim, a front porch that sagged just a wee bit on one side. The lawn's Bermuda grass was the soft yellow of winter, and as a result, made the front yard look neater than it probably might have been. The garden beds were what I called "Dr. Seuss fashion" with branches and dead leaves of tired perennials poking out amidst snow dust. One crooked lamppost leaned toward a patch of bare camellia bushes near the sturdy old wrought iron gate.

I immediately loved the place, just thinking about all the secrets and stories its old walls had seen.

Trudy pushed the gate open with her fancy cane with its red leather handle. The creaking sound from the hinges reminded me of my joints when I got out of bed in the morning—or the portent of something sinister in an old noir. This property was giving all the vibes. I patted my purse, my trusty old folio tucked inside. I would definitely write about this later.

We shuffled up the cracked sidewalk, careful to avoid patches of ice, my head on a swivel as I took in the surroundings. Virginia Marks greeted us at the door, dressed for another decade—long wool skirt, cameo brooch, white hair pulled back into a bun, soft whispies moving around her face, as if trying to escape the severe style.

"Come in, come," Virginia said. Despite her rigid fashion sense, her smile was open and kind. "I am so happy you were able to make it out here." She ushered us inside and closed the door behind us.

"I'm Betty Benino, volunteer for the historical society, as you know. So nice to meet you." I reached out and shook her tiny hand, the skin so thin and fragile. It was also cold, and I put both my hands over hers to give it some warmth.

"The pleasure is all mine, I'm sure," she said, gesturing for us to follow her. "This way."

Her posture was straight, shoulders thrown back, and she moved with grace, almost gliding across the floor, belying her age. She led us through a narrow hallway that smelled like cedar and liniment. My limited view of the interior confirmed a sort of magic to the ancestral home—worn and cobwebbed, yet proud and strong. A threadbare runner lined the hallway, and somewhere nearby, an antique clock ticked steadily, a quiet reminder that time never stopped, even when we did.

In a back room, a library of sorts, amidst boxes and books, she gestured to a cloth-draped frame. "This."

"This is . . .?" Trudy prompted, tapping her cane on the ornate red rug that covered most of the room's wood floor.

I stepped forward. "A painting. May I?" I reached out toward the cloth, waiting for the okay to remove it.

"It's a Holloway," Virginia said, not giving me any indication that I could remove the cloth. "His Winter Garden series. No one's seen it in fifty years. At least not this one."

My breath hitched, and I looked at Trudy, who raised her eyebrows and whispered, "Now that *is* something."

The series was a landscape trio, and two of the paintings were already being prepared for display at the historical society, thanks to a generous donation from a Holloway heir. If Virginia really did have the missing piece, it would finally complete the panorama. For months, no one had been able to say where that third painting had gone. We'd been hoping someone with knowledge would step forward. And here we were.

I touched the cloth. The suspense was about to give me the vapors.

But Virginia waved me off. Disappointment raced through me, and I dropped my hand, stepping back.

"Wait," she said, almost to herself. "I need more time, I think. Maybe one more night just . . . to double check myself. Then I'll show you properly."

*Show us properly?* I nodded, though I didn't know what that meant.

I hesitated, unsure what to say. There was something in Virginia's eyes—a flicker. Trudy had mentioned her tendency toward theatrics, though I still couldn't believe this soft, quiet woman capable of such a thing. Then again, the best actors . . . well, you didn't know they were acting.

"Yes, of course, Virginia," Trudy said. "Whenever you're ready."

"Thank you, dear. You're a true friend."

We retraced our steps to the front door, much to my disappointment. "I'd love a tour of this place," I said to Virginia. "That is, if you're up for it. I just adore old homes."

"I would be happy to honor your request," she said with a single nod of her head. "One day."

*But not today.*

I blew out a loud sigh as we shuffled back through the gate, our boots crunching over gravel and ice.

I glanced over at Trudy, who patted me on the back. "Yeah, I have no earthly idea. Maybe she wanted to warm us up. She's always been a bit of a teaser."

# Chapter Three

By the time I finished wiping down the last sticky tabletop at O'Malley's, I'd already had the uneasy feeling the day was going to go sideways. I just felt out of step after yesterday's visit with Virginia Marks.

"Betty, you're staring again, girlfriend."

I looked up to find Rhonda watching me from behind the bar, one eyebrow arched. She flipped a rag over her shoulder, then poured me a glass of Coca-Cola. Sliding it across the bar, she added, "You clean that table any harder, you're going to sand the varnish right off."

"Sorry," I said, taking the glass. "Just distracted." And then I got distracted by the way the soda bubbled over the ice.

"Dangerous word—distracted," she said, pushing a few of her dark curls out of her face. "Especially since the lunch crowd is about to pour in. But I'm cool if you need to take off. I know this isn't your usual shift. I can totally handle it."

I shook my head. "No way. I'm good." I had offered to work—usually I don't work two days in a row—because I'd wanted to keep busy. These winter months were near about to drive me crazy.

The pub was quiet in that pre-lunch-hour way. A few regulars hunched over their mugs of coffee—I presumed—reading the newspaper, a real one. Some scrolling on their phones. Some talking; some staring at the walls. The low murmur of the radio competed with the clanging of pots and pans back in the kitchen as the cooks prepped for hungry patrons. Wet footprints dotted the old wood flooring; there had been a light snow during the night, and O'Malley's didn't have much for a place to wipe your feet. *I should make a suggestion.*

I circled the rim of the glass with my finger, my mind circling around Virginia Marks and that painting. My hand on the cloth . . .

*I'd been so close.*

Rhonda jammed her hands on her hips. "Don't tell me. Someone lied to you and you're ticked off."

I chuckled. "No, not that."

"Okay, you got scammed, and you're ticked off."

"Never!"

"Has to be . . . hmmm, someone didn't tell you something you know they knew but didn't share, and you're ticked off."

I'd been staring at my glass, but now my head popped up. "That's really close. How did you know?"

She blew on her nails, like she'd just had a manicure. "I'm not just Latina, you know. Got a little fortune-teller blood in me." She bugged out her eyes. "We *know* things."

I was seriously impressed. "I'll keep that in mind for the future." My phone buzzed in my pocket before I could say more.

I glanced at the screen. Trudy.

Talk about a helicopter parent . . .

I stepped away from the bar and answered. "You miss me already?"

There was silence on the other end.

"Trudy?"

"Betty."

This wasn't her usual sassy tone, but okay.

"Trudy." Two could play this game.

"She's dead."

"Who . . .?" But I knew, and a sense of foreboding crept along my spine.

"Virginia Marks is dead," Trudy said, almost a whisper. "They found her this morning."

The room seemed to tilt, just slightly.

"What?" I said. "That . . . that doesn't make sense."

"She was in her garden at the side of the house," Trudy went on, words tumbling now. "Neighbor found her. Called me. Sheriff Brooks is there already. Betty . . ." Her voice dropped. "It doesn't look natural."

I closed my eyes.

Yesterday, Virginia had been standing in her own hallway, perfectly composed, telling us to come back tomorrow.

I looked at Rhonda, who seemed to sense that something was awry. That fortune-teller thing, perhaps. She nodded, giving me permission to go before I'd even had to ask.

"Where are you?"

"At home. I just . . . can't."

"I'll head to Virginia's now," I said.

"Just . . . don't aggravate the sheriff."

*Did that really need to be said?* "I won't," I lied, already reaching for my coat.

# Chapter Four

The drive across town felt longer than usual, every red light popping its big eye to keep me from getting to where I needed to be. Bluejay Ridge looked the same as it always did at lunchtime—shops busy with customers, cars pulling into parking spaces, people walking their dogs dressed in ridiculous sweaters.

Life didn't stop for death. It rarely did.

As I moved toward the mountains, the opposite enveloped me. The serenity in nature's grand space.

The mood changed again as I approached Chestnut Drive.

Yellow tape fluttered near the front gate to Virginia's property, bright and . . . well, just *wrong* against the winter-muted yard. They'd secured the scene. I pulled up to the curb just behind a cruiser.

Sheriff Harlan Brooks stood near the walkway, speaking quietly with one of his deputies. He spotted me immediately and raised a hand—not a wave, exactly. More like he wanted to stop me in my tracks.

Our relationship had improved since my last murder discovery and subsequent snooping. Yet, he seemed to still harbor reservations about my intentions. Why, oh why?

Probably because he would be right. I intended to find out all I could about Virginia's demise—and whether that Holloway painting had anything to do with it.

"Betty," Harlan said as I approached. "This is an active crime scene. You have no business—"

"I know," I said, peering toward the side of the property. "I'll stay right here." I shuffled a bit more to the left for a better view. "I mean here."

He studied me for a moment, then nodded.

As I said, we'd made some progress over the last year.

Leaning over the gate, I put my focus on the side yard. When I saw her, a little sob escaped from somewhere deep inside me.

Virginia lay face up on the stone path near the garden arbor. It was the saddest sight, seeing that sweet old woman so vulnerable and exposed in her death. One arm outstretched. Her head turned away from us. And the snow red beneath her upper back.

I tugged Harlan's shirt sleeve. "She was shot?" I whispered, blurting out the first thing that came to mind, having seen the blood.

He pursed his lips, and I expected he might not say anything at all. But he did.

"Knife."

*Mercy.*

My gaze drifted to the edge of a garden bed, where mountain frost still clung to the soil. A small clump of snowdrops bowed their white heads near her outstretched hand, petals bright against the dark earth. A forensics technician from the county crouched nearby, photographing everything.

"She was holding snowdrops," I said.

Harlan followed my line of sight. "That what those are?"

"Yes. They're one of the first flowers to bloom as winter comes to a close. Beautiful, so delicate."

“Figures you’d know, being the big gardener and all.” He tilted his head, studying me. “You knew her?”

“Not really. I was here yesterday with Trudy. She had a painting she wanted to donate to the historical society. But we never saw it. She said she needed another day to get things in order. Like, she changed her mind last minute and wanted another chance to review her notes. I was crushed. And now this.”

Harlan rocked back on his boot heels and turned his gaze to the crime scene. Because it was a crime scene. Her neck was not sitting the right way—at all. Trudy had warned me, but I hadn’t been fully prepared ... for all this.

I turned away, my heart thumping rapidly. But I couldn’t erase what I’d just seen.

I mourned for the woman . . . and for the promise she hadn’t lived long enough to keep.

Yesterday, Virginia Marks had promised us a donation of a painting. But instead of handing it over, she wanted a little more time.

Today, she was gone, and whatever was on her mind had slipped out of her hands—and ours—perhaps both literally and figuratively.

# Chapter Five

Sheriff Harlan Brooks caught up with me just as I was climbing back into my Jeep.

"Betty."

I paused, one hand still on the door handle. There was something in his tone that told me this wasn't a courtesy check-in to see how I was holding up or a reminder to stay out of trouble. Not that those ever stopped me from doing what I had good mind to do.

"Yes?" I said.

He glanced over his shoulder, back toward the old house on Chestnut Drive, then lowered his voice. "I need to ask you something."

I shut the door and faced him fully. "That sounds ominous."

"Does the name Neville Holloway mean anything to you?"

I opened my mouth, but nothing came out. I'd somehow forgotten that Neville Holloway was the local artist who'd painted intricate landscapes such as the Winter Garden series. I was still in shock over Virginia's demise and would be for some time. But I snapped to. "Oh. Sorry, yes. I mean, at least I know of Holloway. He was a local painter."

"What else do you know?" The deep brown of his eyes bore into mine. He might have been attractive if he wasn't so darn prickly. But I knew he was in cope mode right now, as well he should be.

I folded my arms against the cold. "Virginia mentioned it yesterday. Said the painting she wanted to donate was part of the Holloway Winter Garden series. I wished she'd let Trudy and me see it. That's why we were there, after all. To collect it, I'm pretty sure, and take it to the historical society. The society already has the other two in the trio, donated by the Holloways. But, as I mentioned, she changed her mind at the last minute. Like she wanted to sit with it a little longer."

Harlan nodded slowly, like a man checking off boxes in his mind. The sign of an excellent detective. He certainly had the years in service to have honed the skill. What was it, forty years in various forms of law enforcement? I tried to remember what he'd told me, or maybe Jolene had told me . . .

He broke into my rambling thoughts. "You didn't think that was odd—not showing you the painting? Had she been the one to call you over?"

"Yes. Yes, she'd called Ralph at the historical society, but he's been sick, so then she called Trudy, because they're old friends, their family and all. And Virginia asked that she bring me along, presumably because I volunteer at the society. And then she took us to the back room, which is sort of like a library and storage area, and there was this painting covered by a sheet on an easel. I was hoping for a big reveal." I sighed, my disappointment coming to the fore.

"What was her demeanor like? Especially when she'd decided not to show you the painting?"

"I thought it was theatrical, really" I said, looking off into the distance as I remembered the moment. "Trudy had warned me. Virginia liked a bit of ceremony. I figured she wanted the moment just right. But then again, she could have just been feeling sentimental."

Then something else came to mind, and it must have showed on my face because Harlan asked, "What is it?"

"She told us to come back tomorrow, which is today, and she's dead."

"Mm-hmm," he murmured, scratching the side of his head, where grays were making more of an appearance on his short-cropped curly hair.

Another thought popped into my head. "Did you find the painting?"

He didn't answer right away.

That was answer enough.

"You haven't looked yet," I guessed.

"I'll be right back. Stay put."

So I waited, staying warm in my truck while I made notes in my folio about these new goings-on. My eyes kept veering from the page and back toward the crime scene, watching deputies move in and out of the house.

About thirty minutes later, he returned looking frazzled. I stepped out of the Jeep.

"It's not there," he said. "The easel is empty, the cloth on the floor."

"Maybe she moved it."

"We did a quick sweep of the house and didn't see it. We'll have to do a more in-depth search. She might have put it somewhere to keep it safe, since she'd decided to check herself on . . . maybe provenance and other things she wanted to say about it."

A chill settled somewhere deeper than my coat could reach. "Yes. She wanted to 'show us properly.' Her words."

Harlan exhaled through his nose. "That painting matters, Betty. Whether it's missing because someone took it, or because Virginia hid it, I don't know yet. But if she was killed over it—or over what she knew about it—I need to understand who else might have known it existed."

I stared into the eyes of that achingly beautiful but worn blue house. Of the way Virginia had stood so straight in her hallway, as if holding herself together by will alone.

"She wasn't chatty," I said suddenly. "I don't know any more than what I've told you. Unfortunately. But you're right. If the painting is gone, then we need to know who else knew about it."

"Not we."

I ignored him. "And if someone else new about it, did they take it to preserve it on her behalf, maybe at her request? And they'll come to you sooner than later, once they know Virginia is . . . gone?" I paused. "Or has that painting been flat-out stolen? And that's what got her killed."

"Betty . . ."

I didn't skip a beat. "I don't think she would have told too many people about a painting. She seemed almost secretive about it. It must be quite valuable. I meant to look up the name, Holloway, and do some research. I will now. Harlan—" I finally stopped and looked him in the eye.

He raised an eyebrow in response, adding to the wrinkles embedded in his brown skin. Character, that's what his face had. War wounds from a life lived hard and having seen too much.

I continued. "People like her . . . they have histories. Private ones, maybe, but histories, nonetheless."

"Anyone specific come to mind?"

"Not yet," I said honestly. "But Trudy's known her since childhood. If Virginia talked to anyone, it would've been someone she trusted. I don't suppose it would take much digging—"

"Stop." Harlan held up his hands. "We'll do the digging. You've been a big help, and I appreciate it. If you remember anything else—anything at all—I need you to tell me. But that's the extent of it. You remember something, you come to me, and I will take it from there."

I gave him a look. "You know I will."

"Please let that be the extent of your involvement," he added.

"You can't stop me from researching, Sheriff." I lifted my chin.

"That's what worries me." He touched the brim of his hat. "You can go now, Betty. Stay safe."

I watched him walk back toward the house, the yellow tape snapping softly in the breeze. Then I climbed back into my Jeep and sat there for a long moment, hands resting on the steering wheel.

Virginia Marks had been careful not to just hand off something clearly important to her. She seemed protective—deliberate about her next steps. She was guarding a Holloway painting, but...

Maybe it was something more.

# Chapter Six

The Bluejay Ridge Historical Society met in what used to be a church, one that had long since outgrown its walls and moved up the road. The building now housed glass display cases, folding tables, and the smell of burnt coffee—occupational hazard when meetings went on for too long.

I entered through a pair of stained glass wooden doors to the sound of hushed voices. I didn't have to guess too hard as to the topic.

Virginia Marks had been part of this town her whole life.

Now she wasn't.

But the meeting had been planned long before the terrible incident, and as they say in show biz, "The show must go on." A long table had been set up near the front of the room, scattered with folders, donation forms, and boxes of powdered donuts that no one appeared eager to claim. A large poster board leaned against the wall behind it:

**Bluejay Ridge Historical Society**
**Winter Heritage Fundraiser Celebrating Our History and Community**

About two weeks away. In that moment, I felt like we needed a good two months, at least.

I hung my coat on the back of a chair and slid into a seat

beside Trudy, who was sipping a protein drink, her cane hooked neatly over the table edge.

"Well," she muttered under her breath, "this is cheerful."

Up front, the interim chair—Maybelline Griggs, who had stepped in while Ralph recovered from the flu—cleared her throat and shuffled a stack of papers.

"I know everyone's shaken," she began. "Virginia's loss is . . . well, it's a loss to this town and to this organization. But we do have a rather big decision to make this morning."

That got everyone's attention.

"The event is just around the corner," she continued. "Vendors are booked. Donors are committed. Advertising is out. The question is whether we move forward as planned."

A murmur rippled through the room.

"We should postpone," someone said from the back.

"And lose half our sponsors?" another voice countered. "People have already written checks."

"This doesn't feel right," a third added. "It's too soon."

Trudy leaned toward me. "Virginia would haunt this place if we canceled," she whispered.

I had to admit, I could picture it.

Maybelline held up both hands. "If I may . . ." She cleared her throat, looking uncomfortable in this role. "Let's remember why we're doing this. The roof still leaks. The wiring is still questionable. Climate control is still a dream. If we cancel, we're back to square one."

There was a pause.

Then, from the far side of the table, a familiar, perfectly controlled voice spoke.

"I certainly hope we're not considering canceling."

Priscilla Worthington sat upright at the end of the row,

winter coat draped neatly over her chair, a leather folio open in front of her. Of course she was here. If Bluejay Ridge hosted a ribbon-cutting, garden tour, or bake sale, Priscilla would be somewhere nearby, smiling and quietly running the show.

"Virginia devoted years to this organization," she continued. "If anything, the fundraiser should move forward in her honor."

Several heads nodded.

Priscilla glanced down at her notes. "The Garden Club will still handle the floral installations. I've already confirmed our volunteers. We can adjust the tone—something tasteful, respectful—but there's no reason the event itself should suffer."

That settled the mood more quickly than anything else had.

Maybelline exhaled. "All right, then. Unless there are strong objections, we proceed."

No one objected.

I felt a small, steadying sense of relief. Keeping busy felt better than sitting around waiting for the sadness to settle.

"Now," Maybelline said, consulting another page, "there's one more matter we need to address."

She hesitated.

"We have a guest with us this morning. Dr. Caroline Mercer."

A woman standing near the doorway stepped forward.

She was in her early fifties, maybe, wearing a wool coat the color of slate and practical boots that looked like they'd seen more than one winter. Her hair was pulled back, her expression calm but alert, like someone who had come prepared to work and had no interest in small talk.

"This is the Asheville lady," Trudy murmured under her breath.

Dr. Mercer gave a brief nod to the room. "I understand this is a difficult time," she said. Her voice was clear and direct, without a hint of fuss. "I'm very sorry to hear about Ms. Marks."

Then she folded her hands in front of her.

"I was scheduled to meet with her this morning."

The room went still.

"She contacted me two weeks ago," Mercer continued. "She believed she had a painting that might require professional authentication. I drove down from Asheville today for that purpose."

Maybelline cleared her throat. "The painting she's referring to is . . . currently unaccounted for."

Mercer's expression didn't change, but something sharpened behind her eyes.

"So I've been told," she said. "What I need to know is who else was aware that Ms. Marks possessed this piece."

A few people shifted in their chairs.

I felt Trudy glance at me.

Priscilla spoke first. "Virginia mentioned it to me several weeks ago. In general terms. She said she might be contributing something special to the fundraiser."

Mercer nodded once.

"Anyone else?"

Maybelline raised a hand. "She told Ralph before he got sick. He was planning to coordinate the exhibit space to go with the other Holloway—" She stopped and slapped a hand to her mouth. "Should I be sharing this?"

"Oh please." Trudy swished her hand in the air as she

pushed herself to standing with the help of her cane. "If it's not known by most of us already, it'll be known soon. She had the third Holloway painting that would have completed the trio. As we all know, Joyce Holloway was so very generous to donate two of her grandfather Neville Holloway's paintings to the society, in honor of this town and the beauty within it. These two paintings are part of a trio, again as most of us know. Virginia had what she believed was the third painting and had planned to donate it, to complete the picture, shall we say. She called me yesterday and asked me to bring Betty over to her house to look at it."

Several heads turned our way as Trudy took a seat.

I straightened a little. "We didn't actually see it," I said. "The painting was covered. She said she wanted one more night to review her notes before showing it to us."

Mercer's attention settled fully on me.

"Did she say why?"

"Just wanted more time with it, is what she said," I said. "Maybe wanted to double check provenance or maybe was second guessing the donation. It is my understanding these paintings are quite valuable . . . although that's what you're here for." I gestured toward our visitor.

Mercer's mouth tightened slightly. "She didn't give me many details," she said. "She asked me to confirm authenticity and give her a sense of current market value. She also mentioned the painting was part of Neville Holloway's Winter Garden series, though I've yet to confirm."

The room leaned in, almost without realizing it.

"What does that mean, exactly?" Maybelline asked.

"If the painting is what she described," Mercer said

carefully, "then it could indeed be the missing work from that series. One piece has been unaccounted for . . . for a long, long time."

A quiet murmur moved around the table.

"If Ms. Marks did, in fact, have that painting," Mercer went on, "it would be of significant value."

"How significant?" someone asked.

"Museum-level," Mercer said.

That word hung in the air, and I felt my stomach dip.

Trudy let out a low whistle. Priscilla's pen stopped moving.

"And," Mercer added, "any time a work of that value surfaces after decades, there are usually questions about its history. Where it's been. How it changed hands."

"You're saying someone else might think it belongs to them?" Maybelline asked.

"I'm saying," Mercer replied evenly, "that high-value works attract attention. Collectors, attorneys, institutions. And it should. It just has to be authenticated and valued, which is why I am here."

The room went very still.

"You're saying someone else might think it belongs to them?" Maybelline asked.

"I'm saying," Mercer replied evenly, "that when a work of that value surfaces after decades, questions follow."

I thought about Virginia standing in her hallway the day before, so composed, so deliberate.

One more night.

"What exactly did she tell you?" I asked.

Mercer looked at me again, measuring.

"She said," Mercer replied slowly, "that if the documentation confirmed her suspicions, the painting might change a few long-standing assumptions about its ownership."

A shiver moved down my arms.

"Did she seem worried?" I asked.

Mercer paused.

"Yes," she said.

That word landed heavier than anything else she'd said.

Maybelline cleared her throat. "Well. Given the circumstances, we'll... we'll continue our efforts to locate the painting and coordinate with the sheriff's office."

Mercer nodded. "Please do. And if it's recovered, I'd like to examine it as soon as possible."

She glanced around the room once more.

"In the meantime, I would advise discretion. If word spreads about a piece of this significance, it won't just attract local interest."

She didn't need to finish the sentence.

Everyone understood.

Collectors.

Lawyers.

People with long memories.

The meeting moved on after that—vendor confirmations, catering adjustments, who would rewrite the opening program to include a tribute to Virginia. I made notes where I needed to, answered a few questions about the exhibit scripts, and tried to focus on the logistics in front of me.

But my mind kept circling back to the same thing.

Virginia hadn't just been preparing a donation.

She'd been preparing for a revelation.

When the meeting finally broke up, people gathered their

papers and drifted toward the coffee table, voices rising now that decisions had been made.

Trudy nudged my elbow. "Well," she said quietly, "that just got bigger."

"Much bigger," I agreed.

Across the room, Dr. Mercer spoke briefly with Maybelline, then closed her notebook and headed toward the door.

I hesitated.

Then I went after her.

"Dr. Mercer?"

She turned.

"I'm Betty Benino," I said. "I was with Trudy yesterday when Virginia showed us the painting."

"Covered," Mercer said.

"Covered," I confirmed. "But she seemed very protective of it."

Mercer studied me for a moment. "She was."

"Do you think someone else knew what it was?" I asked.

Mercer considered that.

"If Ms. Marks shared her concerns with anyone beyond this organization," she said carefully, "then yes. It's possible."

She opened the door and paused.

"One more thing," she added. "When she called me, she said something that stuck with me."

I waited.

"She said, 'If this turns out the way I think it will, some people aren't going to be happy to see it come back into the light.'"

Mercer gave a small nod and stepped outside into the cold.

I stood there for a moment, my hand still on the doorframe.

Come back into the light.

Behind me, voices rose again as people talked about centerpieces and seating charts and donation baskets.

The fundraiser would go on.

But for the first time, it crossed my mind that the missing painting might matter to more people than Virginia had ever intended.

And some of them might not want it found.

# Chapter Seven

If there was one place in Bluejay Ridge where the truth eventually surfaced, it wasn't the sheriff's office, the church, or even Millie's Bakery.

It was the nail salon.

Gloss & Glow sat in a little strip center just off Main Street, sandwiched between a boutique that sold aggressively cheerful seasonal décor and a tax preparation office that looked like it hadn't been updated since the Reagan administration. Inside, the air smelled faintly of acetone and lavender, and the low hum of conversation blended with the whir of foot spas and the click of nail tools.

Jolene was already settled into one of the massage chairs when I walked in, her shoes kicked off, her feet soaking in a basin of swirling pink water.

"Well, there she is," she called. "Come on, Tater. I already told them you were coming."

Of course she had.

I hung my coat on the rack and slid into the chair beside her. A young woman in a neat black apron handed me a color wheel and smiled.

"Your usual?" she asked.

I blinked at her. "Do I have a usual?"

She frowned just a smidge, as if I had disappointed her so many times. "You have many, I know. But I think the soft pink. Good? It looks like you are not wearing anything, but you are."

"Good," I said. I needed some softness right now. I was feeling tender.

Jolene leaned over, lowering her voice even though half the room was already talking at full volume.

"You look like you didn't sleep," she said.

"I slept," I said. "My brain didn't."

"Same," she replied. "This whole Virginia thing has everybody stirred up."

The technician lifted my feet into the warm water, and I let out a small sigh before I could stop myself.

"Okay," Jolene said, settling back into her chair like she was preparing for a proper visit. "Tell me what happened at the meeting today. I haven't had a chance to get the 411 from Trudy."

So I shared.

I told her about the decision to move forward with the fundraiser. Dr. Mercer and her practical clothes and tense hair and no-nonsense voice. And the part about the painting.

Jolene's perfect eyebrows shot straight up. "My word! Museum level?"

"That's what she said."

"We're going to need guards!" The lady at the station across from us looked up, alarmed. Jolene shrugged, smiled, and gave her a finger wave. "Just kidding!"

My nail tech began working on my left foot, and I focused on the steady, gentle motion while Jolene leaned a little closer.

"You know what else?" she said quietly. "Virginia wasn't acting like herself the last couple weeks."

"Wait—you know her? How did I not know this?"

"Not personally, but enough to get included in all the tittle-tattle. Plus, she's been Trudy's friend for a long time."

Jolene never ceased to amaze me as a resource. "Okay," I said, nodding. "So how was Virginia acting different lately?"

"Hmmm." She tapped her chin. "Not nervous exactly but distracted. I heard she went to the Baptist church over near the mountains last Sunday, and she didn't even stay for the social afterward."

"Doesn't seem like a big deal. Who did you hear this from? Was it really that big of a deal?"

Jolene shook her head. "Maybe not. But Lila—you know, Rhonda's cousin who does hair out of her house on Chestnut—heard about it from one of the other neighbors, a customer of hers. *And* something else."

That caught my attention. "What else?"

She pursed her lips with a sly look. "This other neighbor saw headlights in Virginia's driveway the night she died. Somebody got out and walked up. To. The. Porch!"

My stomach tightened. "Who?"

"No idea," Jolene said. "She didn't recognize the person, or if it was even a man or a woman or a big kid! Just a dark shape and lights in the drive. This neighbor, Tenny, figured it was just a rare visitor or maybe a late delivery, and she didn't think much of it until the news hit."

The technician switched to my other foot, and I watched the water ripple as she adjusted the basin.

"The night before," I said softly.

The night Virginia wanted one more look at her notes.

The night before they found her—dead.

"Did Tenny tell the sheriff?" I asked.

"Lila said she did," Jolene said, making a face. "But you know how that goes. 'Didn't get a good look, probably nothing, don't want to bother anybody.'"

*Could've been nothing. Could've been everything.*

Jolene studied my face. "You're going to pop a screw loose."

"I'm thinking whoever showed up that night didn't come for tea talk."

Jolene nodded once, lips pressed together.

The technician began trimming my nails, and for a few minutes the only sounds were the soft snip of clippers and the low murmur of other conversations drifting around the room.

Finally, Jolene spoke again.

"Well," she said, "if that painting is worth what that Mercer woman says, I guarantee you it's not just the people in this town who'd be interested in it."

"That's what worries me," I said. "Even if her death and the painting aren't related, it's still a big deal. The sooner the historical society can get hold of it and institute security measures, the better. It's what Virginia wanted. It belongs here."

We paid at the front and stepped back out into the cold, the winter air biting at our ankles where our jeans had ridden up.

For a moment we stood there, pulling on our coats.

"Lunch?" Jolene asked.

"I've got a shift at O'Malley's later," I said. "But I've got time for a quick soup at the new place."

She knew exactly what I was talking about. "Let's do it."

The Urban Grind was one of those upscale deals that didn't quite fit into our laid-back vibe. I mean, we could hardly call ourselves "urban," but I respected their clever use of words.

We crossed the street, the wind picking up just enough to make me wish I'd worn thicker socks.

The Urban Grind sat in a short strip center wedged between an insurance agency and an empty storefront that had turned over three times in the past year. Inside the café, everything gleamed—polished concrete floors, metal stools, a menu board written in looping chalk.

I glanced around as we stepped in.

Ralph Jenkins sat near the window, a bowl of soup in front of him.

Jolene lifted a hand in a small wave. “Well, I’ll be,” she murmured.

Ralph looked up and gave a quick nod, but he didn’t smile. Didn’t motion us over, either. Which was fine by me. I didn’t need whatever bug he was carrying. I gave a polite wave of my own, then turned toward the counter.

A thought hit me. Why was he here among the living if he had the flu?

Too sick to attend meetings. Too sick to do much of anything—enough that we’d had to bring in Maybelline to fill his role in the interim.

And yet here he was.

Out. Having lunch. Not looking especially spry, but still ...

I didn’t say anything, but something about it didn’t sit quite right.

# Chapter Eight

I've learned a thing or two about a thing or two when it comes to Sheriff Harlan Brooks, and one of those things is this: he doesn't invite people along for the ride.

So when he called early in the day and said, "You busy right now?" I knew two things right away.

One, he already had somewhere in mind.

And two, whatever it was mattered.

"I was going to put in some time for the historical society fundraiser. Lots of boring but important jobs to be checked off. But I'd pretty much rather be doing anything but that. I can peel off some time." I told him. "What have you got in mind?"

Of course he didn't answer the question. "Good," he said. "Meet me at the station. And wear shoes you don't mind getting dirty."

I put on my gardening boots and headed that way.

---

Fifteen minutes outside the town proper and over the highway, the pavement ended.

Harlan's steel blue Ford Bronco turned onto a narrow gravel road that began climbing into the mountains, the town dropping away behind us. Houses thinned, then disappeared entirely, replaced by bare hardwoods, rock outcroppings, and patches of old snow tucked into the shade.

"This feels promising," I said, gripping the door handle as we hit a rut.

"You wanted history," Harlan said. "This is where it lives."

The road narrowed again, then opened into a small clearing.

A cabin sat at the edge of it.

Not "cottagecore" cabin. Definitely a "backwoods and no air-conditioning" cabin. Weathered boards. A metal stovepipe sending up a thin line of smoke. But it wasn't a pile of junk either. There was an organized vibe to it all. A truck parked in between a three-sided rectangle made of logs, filled with gravel. A neat stack of split wood along the side wall. Tools that actually got used leaned against the porch rail, and a set of wind chimes made from carved wood tapped softly in the cold air.

"An actual outhouse?" I laughed lightly and pointed at the small outhouse off to the side.

Harlan didn't laugh. Or even comment.

"Oh," I said, realizing it was the real deal—and used as such.

Harlan shut off the engine.

"You sure this man's expecting us?" I asked.

"He's expecting me."

We stepped out, the pines and hardwoods surrounding us on all sides. Not claustrophobic—just nature doing its thing. The air felt sharper up here, and I sucked in a lungful.

Two hound dogs lay on the porch. One with its head between its paws, peering at us with one eye. The other, smaller, showed a little more interest with a thump of its tail.

"That's Dog and Girl," Harlan said.

"Some mighty fine names." I let out a small laugh, but honestly, the names felt just right here in this setting.

Before we reached the porch, the door opened.

The man who stepped outside looked like he was right where he was supposed to be. Here. In this cabin. On this quiet plot of land.

Tall but stooped, shoulders still broad under a worn canvas jacket. White hair and beard growing wild. Thin, with deep lines carved into his dark leathery face, like bark on a tree. His eyes, though, were steady and clear. Just like Harlan's.

"Harlan," he said.

"Uncle Earl."

They shook hands once.

Harlan nodded toward me. "This is Betty Benino. Historical Society."

Earl tipped his head.

"Ma'am."

Then he turned and went inside without another word. We followed. Dog and Girl did not.

The two-room cabin smelled like wood smoke and cedar. Everything looked handmade—bowls, walking sticks, a heavy kitchen table scarred from years of use, stools for seats around it. A small fire burned in a woodstove. Two worn recliners faced the fire, a circle of wood on three legs forming a small table in between. More tools lined the walls and most of the open setting-down spaces, ready to work the soil or chop a tree or whittle a figurine.

Earl poured coffee into three mismatched mugs and placed them on the kitchen table without asking. Harlan grabbed two and handed me one, then gestured for me to take a seat in the recliner. I did, though I sat on the very edge. I didn't want to sink too far in and not be able to get out without help. With my short stature, it has happened before.

Harlan pulled up a stool so we formed a circle around the fire.

Earl didn't sit in the other recliner right away. Instead, he used a poker to shift the coals, watching the fire settle before lowering himself onto a stool.

"What's come loose?" he asked.

"You remember the Holloways?"

Earl's hand stopped on the mug.

Apparently that was answer enough because Harlan continued. "One of Neville's paintings turned up. Winter Garden series."

"Just one?"

"Two have been donated to the historical society," I chimed in, though neither man looked at me. "By Joyce Holloway. Such a nice thing to do. I mean, legacy matters, right? So, this is the third one—"

Harlan cut me off. "Belonged to Virginia Marks."

Earl just stared at the fire for a long few seconds. Then, "And now she's dead."

I glanced at Harlan. Neither of us had mentioned that. Or was there some secret code between these two men?

Earl finally looked at me. "Word travels," he added by way of explanation.

He took a slow sip of coffee.

Silence filled our space.

"Gonna be problems."

I leaned forward. "Oh? Why is that?"

Earl didn't answer right away. He sat on a stool and set his mug on the table. The *thud* from the mug hitting the wood seemed to echo. He folded his hands together.

"Holloways and Halfords," he said.

Harlan's jaw tightened. "Old trouble."

Earl gave a single nod. "Old. Not gone."

Harlan glanced my way. "Up past the second ridge," he said, "before they started slicing up the land, the Holloways were on one side, the Halfords on the other."

"Lots of land," Earl added. "Just the same, folks don't like to share."

He reached for the poker, nudging the stove door open. Orange light spilled across the floorboards.

"Men in suits came 'round with their rolled papers," he went on. "Lines on maps. Lines on deeds. Lines in people's heads."

"Surveyors?" I asked.

"Lawyers. Bank men. All the same, far as I care," Earl said. "After that, nothing stayed simple."

He let the door fall shut again.

Harlan barely moved; he just watched him. "You remember the paintings?"

Earl's gaze moved from the fire to Harlan, then to me.

"Them winter scenes hung on the Holloway wall when I was a boy," he said, a faraway look in his eyes. "Three of 'em. Made you feel like the snow was right there in the room."

My chest tightened a little. Hearing him describe them made the missing piece feel like a hole in Bluejay Ridge's tapestry. I wanted—needed—to see all three together, the way they were meant to be.

"Years later," Earl continued, "Halfords had 'em."

"The paintings, you mean?" I asked. "They bought the series from Holloway or his heirs?"

He shrugged. "A deal."

"A sale?" I tried again. I really did have to learn how to talk "Earl."

"Depends who you ask," he said.

Harlan stepped in. "Holloway side called them stolen. Halford side called them owed. Do I remember that right, Uncle Earl?"

"Yup."

Harlan's mouth flattened. "Both families claimed the series as theirs."

"Mm." Earl took a sip of coffee.

"Let me see if I've got this straight," I said slowly. "Holloways had all three. Then the Halfords had all three. Everybody argued over how that happened."

"Sounds right," Harlan said. "And somewhere in there, it stopped being about art and started being about whose wall they were on."

"Brushstrokes didn't matter," Earl added.

"Family feuds," Harlan said quietly.

"Several feuds," Earl replied.

"Holloways got two back in the end," Harlan went on. "But the one—"

"Middle one," Earl clarified.

"—went missing."

Earl took another sip, then smacked his lips softly. "Mmm-hm. Gone."

Harlan looked at me. "And it's been missing ever since."

"Until Virginia," I whispered.

The stove cracked softly as a log shifted.

I thought of Virginia—how she'd wanted one more night with the painting and her notes before handing it over. What had been going through her mind? I wished now I'd asked more questions during my one visit to her home.

"I don't know how she came to get it," I said slowly, "but if she really does have that missing piece, someone might have decided that was a problem."

Earl's hooded eyes landed on me. "Some folks don't like old things resurfacing," he said. "'specially if they think it proves 'em wrong."

A little shiver walked down my arms.

"Is it just about the paintings?" I asked, remembering the bit about lines and papers. It sounded like those two families might have argued about anything and everything. "Or is there more to it?"

Earl took a breath and let it out through his nose.

"Up here, things get tied together," he said.

Harlan jumped in again. "Names. Land. Promises made on porches after dark. Those pictures were in the room for more than one of those talks, I'd wager. Tied by a single thread. And if someone pulls on that thread . . ."

"You tug loose a whole lotta trouble," Earl finished.

Silence settled in the room, thicker than the smoke.

"I know Joyce Holloway is still around," I said. "Having donated two of the trio. Any of the Halford kin still up this way?"

"Some," Earl said. "Scattered. Some pretend they don't care about old business no more. Some do."

He studied me then, not unkindly, but the intensity of his stare still unnerved me.

"Ask too many questions," he said, "you wake up memories. And those ain't ever as tidy as folks think."

He sniffed and pulled his coat tighter around his body.

"I'll leave you be now, Uncle Earl," Harlan said, standing. "You need anything?"

"Got everything I need right here." Earl rose, joints creaking, and walked us to the door.

We stood on the porch for a moment, taking in the trees and the narrow track of road that had brought us here. Dog and Girl got up, gave us a quick sniff, and I patted their heads. Then they meandered down the steps and into the woods.

The wind moved through the branches, a low rush around the cabin walls.

And for the first time, the Holloway painting felt like not just a missing piece of art, but an old argument.

One that had been waiting a long time to start again.

# Chapter Nine

The drive home took me along the familiar curve of Lake Pointe Road, past neat rows of cottages and tidy winter gardens waiting for spring. A few houses had gone full Leprechaun—clovers and pots of gold and rainbow banners everywhere. I'd opted for a simple wreath on my porch post, one I'd made myself and filled with dried orange slices, suet nuggets, acorns, walnut halves, and plenty of fresh greenery—little treats for the birds and squirrels, and maybe a little hedge against bad luck too.

I pulled into my driveway and parked, hands resting on the steering wheel for a moment. I felt the pinch of paranoia, and that bothered me. What did I have to be paranoid about?

I got out of the Jeep and held my keys strategically between each finger, like a weapon. I walked around the yard for a moment. Same cottages. Same lake peeking through the trees beyond the back fences. Same neighborly bubble I'd grown to know and love.

Except now part of that bubble had a missing painting and a dead woman lodged in it like a splinter.

When I stepped inside, the house was warm and familiar, and I felt relief wash through me. Nutty hopped onto the front windowsill and chittered something that sounded suspiciously like scolding, then vanished again.

"I was gone three hours," I told him, even though he was out of sight. "You'll live."

I grabbed a handful of peanuts and tossed them onto the porch, then set my bag down next to the sofa. For a moment I just stood there in the middle of the living room, looking around.

Nothing out of place. No sense that anything had been disturbed.

But that warm and familiar feeling had been replaced by a sense that someone was standing right there with me.

"Salvy?" I said softly, thinking—just for a second—of my late husband.

A knock at the front door made me jump.

I crossed the room and opened it.

Trudy and Jolene stood on the porch like the Ghosts of Gossip Present. Trudy wore a quilted navy jacket; Jolene had on a hot pink puffer that could probably be seen from space. Jolene held a casserole dish wrapped in a checkered towel.

"I don't know why I made this again," she said, lifting it a little, "but I've had my fill. The rest is yours. Chicken and rice with extra cheese, still warm."

"I'm here for the coffee," Trudy announced.

"By all means." I waved them in.

Jolene set the dish on the pass-through and peeled back the towel. I got a whiff, and my stomach rumbled. She brushed her hands off and turned, giving me a once-over.

"You've got your thinking face on," she said.

"I always have my thinking face on."

"You were with Harlan today," Trudy said, easing herself into a chair at the kitchen table. "Went to see his Uncle Earl."

Like she was the Oracle or something.

"I did," I said, grabbing mugs for the coffee. "It was . . . unexpected. And interesting."

"Interesting how?" Jolene asked, already pulling out chairs and making herself at home.

After putting the casserole in the oven on low to keep it warm, I set the timer, Keurig'd three coffees, and took a seat with them at the table.

"Okay," I said, lowering my voice out of habit, even though it was just us. "Short version: tiny mountain cabin, big woodstove, man of very few words who somehow knows everything, including the Holloway paintings."

Trudy's eyes sharpened. "Oh, this sounds promising. Go on."

I went into more detail to tickle all the senses, my writerly instincts in go mode. I told them about the trip up the mountain. About Earl and his cabin. About how he'd seen the paintings hanging on the Holloway wall. How later they were moved to the Halford home. The back-and-forth ownership arguments. How the series went from art to ammunition in a family standoff. And how, in the end, two of the paintings found their way back to the Holloways . . . but the middle one vanished.

"Do you remember the name Halford?" I finished. As I asked it, the name started floating in my mind's eye. I'd seen it somewhere.

"I sure do. But I don't know why," Trudy said, frowning as she thought.

Jolene shot her hand up. "I know, I know."

"This isn't a classroom, but we appreciate your decorum to wait your turn," Trudy said dryly.

Jolene brought her hand down and smiled so big her entire face squished. "They are members of the historical society, silly. The son and daughter—or maybe that should be grandson and granddaughter, depending how you do the tree. Laurel Halford and her little brother, Beau. Laurel's the one who does most of the talking. Beau's the quiet one."

And just like that, it clicked.

"They are," I said. "How could I have missed that?"

"Might want to check in with your doctor," Trudy quipped.

"I'm sharp as a tack, thank you very much."

Trudy waved a hand. "Sharp things rust too, you know."

The oven timer chimed. *Saved by the ding.* I got up, slid the casserole out of the oven, and made a dish for Trudy and me. Jolene passed with a hard no.

We ate at the table, the conversation drifting to safer ground—fundraiser details, centerpieces, whether Priscilla's idea of "simple winter elegance" was going to require more volunteer hours than anyone wanted.

But even while we talked, my attention kept drifting toward the front window, to the quiet little street where nothing ever happened. Hopefully it would stay that way.

# Chapter Ten

Wrapping my apron around my waist, I stepped through the back employee entrance of O'Malley's for a rare evening shift. The pub was already buzzing, the dinner crowd filling the booths and barstools. The familiar clatter of dishes, low hum of conversation, and soft classic rock from the speakers settled me after the spooked-out vibe I got back at home.

"Hey, Detective," Rhonda called out.

"Retired," I deadpanned.

"Sure you are."

Chuckling, I grabbed an order pad and got down to business. The rhythm of the work pulled me along—drinks, orders, refills, quick jokes, small-town catchup. Just the medicine I needed.

Halfway through the shift, Tootie slid onto a stool at the end of the bar, shedding her coat and fluffing that gorgeous red hair, then securing it into a ponytail.

"What a nice surprise," I said, setting a napkin in front of her. "Hot date?"

She giggled. "No, just me," she said. "It's my hydration therapy."

"The best kind of therapy. What'll ya have?"

"I could do with a glass of white and your special today. I love the po' boys here."

"Excellent choice. Be right—"

The front door swung open, and two men walked in.

My first thought was that they didn't look like locals. Tootie turned to have a look and said, "They're not from around here." And soon, everyone in the place was watching the strangers as they paused just inside the doorway.

One man wore a charcoal wool coat and fancy loafers. He had big city written all over him. His shoulders were back, chest out, and his eyes—sharp as a bird's—moved quickly around the room.

The other was shorter, wearing a blue suit with a red tie slightly askew. His pale face and soft edges told me he wasn't a gym rat or even an outdoor enthusiast of any kind. A desk and a computer screen were his comfort zones.

Grand entrance made, they headed straight for the bar.

Rhonda wiped her hands on a towel. "Evening, gentlemen. What can I get you?"

The taller man gave a polite nod. "Actually, we're looking for someone."

She crossed her arms. "Oh yeah? Who would that be?"

"Betty Benino."

It was as if someone had turned off the room's volume with a flip of a switch.

Tootie slowly turned her head toward me. "So, um," she said under her breath, "what did you do now?"

"I wish I knew," I muttered.

I smoothed my apron and walked toward them, doing my best to keep my expression neutral.

"I'm Betty."

Both men turned to face me.

"Ms. Benino," the taller one said. "My name is Mark Delaney. This is Thomas Reed. We're with Reed, Delaney & Associates from Atlanta."

"Long drive," I said.

"Yes, ma'am. We represent the Halford heirs."

My stomach gave a small, unpleasant dip.

"And we were given your name by Dr. Caroline Mercer and by the historical society. We were told you might be working tonight."

Behind me, I could feel Tootie sit up a little straighter on her stool.

Rhonda didn't move away. If anything, she moved closer.

"What is Reed, Delaney & Associates, exactly?" I asked.

"We're attorneys, ma'am," Delaney said.

"And what's this about?" I kept my voice even. Calm. The whole bar was watching, whether they meant to be or not.

"We understand you were assisting the late Virginia Marks with documentation and exhibit preparation for a painting she recently identified." Delaney's tone was the epitome of professional, and it came across like he was reciting memorized lines.

"Hardly," I said. "We never got that far."

"But that was the plan," he clarified.

I shrugged.

Thomas Reed opened a slim leather portfolio and glanced at a page inside, though he didn't offer it up.

"Our firm represents the surviving heirs of the Halford estate," Delaney continued. "Laurel Halford and her brother, Beau. Dr. Mercer informed us that the work Ms. Marks described may be part of the original Halford holdings."

"This is hardly the place to discuss legal matters," I said.

"This won't take much longer," Delaney said.

Rhonda leaned in, her smile 100 percent fake. "Either buy

a drink like everybody else or keep it moving. We're not doing a courtroom scene in my bar."

Neither man reacted.

Impressive self-control, honestly. Like robots almost.

I took a breath. "Here's what I can tell you. I don't have the painting. I never saw it uncovered. Virginia wanted one more night before donating it. Then she was murdered, and the painting went missing."

Reed's pen moved across the page in his notebook.

"Do you happen to know what research materials Ms. Marks was working from?" Delaney asked. "Correspondence, ownership records, anything of that nature?"

"No idea," I said.

Reed wrote that down too.

Delaney cleared his throat. "We're not here to complicate the situation, Ms. Benino."

"It's not my situation to be complicated," I said, keeping my tone controlled. "You should be speaking with Ralph Jenkins. He's the president of the historical society."

"We were told Mr. Jenkins is still recovering from illness."

"I'm sure he can take a phone call."

He continued as if I hadn't spoken. "And Mrs. Maybelline Griggs suggested that since Ms. Marks had been working directly with you and Dr. Mercer on the exhibit materials, you might have the most current information regarding the painting's location and documentation."

*Oh, Maybelline.* I resisted the urge to rub my temples.

"If this is the missing Winter Garden piece," Delaney said, "the ownership history may be subject to formal review."

"Lawyer language," Rhonda murmured, but loud enough

to carry. I heard snickers coming from the back corner of the room.

"Our clients' position," Delaney said evenly, "is that any property removed from the Halford estate without proper transfer remains part of the family holdings."

I thought of Earl and the way he'd said, *Gonna be problems.*

"Well," I said, "right now the painting isn't with the historical society. Or me. Or anywhere I know of at this time. As far as I know, the sheriff's office is treating its disappearance as part of an active investigation. Sheriff Harlan Brooks. Give him a call."

"If the work is recovered," Reed said, speaking for the first time, "we would appreciate being notified before any public exhibition or transfer takes place."

"I really have no control over that. Now, unless you'd like to order something . . ." I let the sentence hang.

Rhonda lifted her eyebrows as if to say, *Choose wisely.*

"Thank you, Ms. Benino," Delaney said. "We may be in touch again, depending on what the investigation turns up."

"I'm not—"

But they'd already turned for the door, their polished shoes gliding across the wooden floor without a sound.

The pub noise swelled back to normal as soon as the door closed behind them, like someone had un-muted the room.

Tootie slid off her stool and came straight over. "I heard about Virginia's passing," she said. "But sounds like you're going to have to fill me in on all the rest. This sounds almost scandalous."

"That's one way to look at it."

I looked toward the front of the pub, where the night pressed dark against the glass.

Earl had been right. The Holloway wasn't just valuable. It had been the reason for family feuds—ones that clearly weren't finished. And the lawyer angle certainly kicked it up a notch or two.

*Mercy.* This was going to get uglier than a mud fence.

# Chapter Eleven

I parked at the curb in front of the Historical Society and slid out of my Jeep. The air seemed different this morning. Like spring was hovering nearby, tapping its foot, waiting for winter to stop being a jerk and move on. I took a big inhale and savored the moment.

But I also knew that winters in the Georgia mountains were stubborn. They lingered. They teased. They came back for one more visit like a guest who'd already said goodbye at the door and then remembered they forgot their casserole dish.

*Come on, springtime. I'm cheering for you, and so is my garden.*

Inside, the building was already busy. Bodies bustling. Voices floating. Papers shuffling. A small group stood near the coat rack, debating about whether we should call the fundraiser "Winter Heritage" or "Late Winter Heritage," as if renaming the season could make the weather behave.

I slipped past a display of antique quilting squares and found Maybelline Griggs in the meeting room. She stood over the long table with a stack of folders, a pen behind one ear, and the expression of a woman who had not asked for this job but was going to do it anyway.

Maybelline looked relieved to see me. "Betty," she said. "Good. Come sit. Before I lose my mind and start filing everything by astrology sign."

"I'd actually respect that," I told her, pulling out a chair. "Some of these donors are definitely Pisces."

It made no sense, really, but Maybelline gave a tight smile anyway. I took a seat opposite her, and she slid a folder across the table.

"We got a letter," she said.

"The lawyers?" I guessed.

She nodded. "Very official. Kinda cold, really. I mean, a woman did just die, people! Act right." Her voice pitched higher with each word.

I reached out and patted her hand, then skimmed the letter. It was much of the same I'd heard the night before, only more official and even a tad . . . threatening?

Claims. Interests. Holdings. Transfer. Review.

I set it down carefully, like it might bite.

"Well," I said, "that's cheerful."

Maybelline massaged her temples. "Ralph is still out.

Doctor says he needs rest, and I'm not about to argue with a doctor. But it means every question comes to me. Every complaint comes to me. And everyone keeps asking me where the painting is like I've got it hidden in my purse."

"Priscilla probably thinks you do," I said.

Maybelline's eyes flicked up. "Priscilla has opinions about everything right now. *I can't even* with that woman."

"That's because she's Priscilla," I said. "She'd have opinions during a tornado."

Maybelline exhaled. "And now we've got lawyers sending letters like they want to take over our town and boss us all around."

A wet cough sounded from behind me.

Maybelline froze. I turned.

Ralph Jenkins appeared in the doorway in an old cardigan sweater—and slippers on his feet. His face was pale, his eyes a little manic, and his hair had that slept-on look. In one hand he held a paper cup with URBAN GRIND stamped on the side.

"Ralph," Maybelline said, half relief and half alarm. "What are you doing here? Your doctor said—"

"My doctor doesn't run this building," he snapped, then immediately coughed and winced like his own voice offended him. He shuffled in, set the cup down, and stared at the letter on the table. "I leave for three days, and Atlanta starts making demands."

"Ralph," Maybelline warned.

He lifted a hand, like he couldn't decide whether he wanted to calm her down or silence her. "We are not going to let this turn into a spectacle," he said, voice rough. "Not in here. Not two weeks before the fundraiser. Not with Virginia—" He stopped short, swallowed hard. "Not after what happened."

My stomach tightened. "By chance, did Virginia talk to you before . . . you know . . ."

Ralph's gaze flicked to me. Away. Back. "Virginia, um, called. Yes," he said, and the pause before the word *called* was loud as a bell.

Maybelline's posture went rigid. "Oh my. Have you told the sheriff?"

He let loose a long stretch of coughs, then a sneeze, after which he wiped his nose with his sweater sleeve. I stood up and took two steps back. Maybelline covered her face with the legal documents. He waved it off like the coughing was merely an inconvenience. "She left a message. On the office phone."

My skin prickled. "When?"

Ralph's jaw worked. "Late. The night before."

"And you . . .?" Maybelline started.

"I listened," he said quickly, then shook his head. "I mean, I only listened to it once. I was half-delirious. I couldn't tell what was the flu and what was . . . her."

"That's not an answer," Maybelline said, tone sharp.

Ralph bristled. "Well, it's the truth."

But I wasn't so sure. Not because it didn't make sense. Because it sounded like he'd practiced that answer.

"What did she say?" I asked.

"I'm not repeating it in the middle of a meeting room."

"Please tell me you shared this with Sheriff Brooks," Maybelline said.

His nostrils flared. "I don't have to tell you anything. Or anyone else, for that matter—we're not going to hand over every file and scrap of paper in this place to people who don't know our history." He pressed his hand to his mouth as if to suppress another cough. But it didn't work.

I took another casual step away from him. Why was he even here?

"Ralph, if I may, you should be in bed," I said. "You're clearly still in the throes."

He didn't respond, and Maybelline stared at him like she'd just met a different man wearing Ralph's face.

Ralph waved both hands in front of him. "Relax, ladies. I'll tell Harlan," he said, too fast. "I will. I just—" He glanced toward his office. "I need a minute."

He turned and started down the hall.

"He needs more than a minute," I said.

Maybelline looked at me, her expression tight. "Dr. Mercer asked to speak with you," she said, like she was forcing herself back into a task list before she said something she couldn't take back. "She's in Ralph's office."

*Of course she is.*

# Chapter Twelve

Ralph's office was small and overstuffed, with framed photos of Bluejay Ridge from decades past—black-and-white shots of the courthouse square, men in suspenders posing beside an old truck, women standing proudly with baskets of apples.

Mercer looked mildly out of place in the room, like someone had dropped a legal document into a scrapbook.

She stood near the window, coat folded over one arm, her posture straight and efficient as ever. She turned when I entered.

"Ms. Benino," she said. "Thank you for coming."

"Betty," I corrected automatically. "Everyone calls me Betty."

Mercer gave a short nod. "I won't take much of your time," she said, getting right to it. "I'm concerned about Ms. Marks's papers."

"I have no knowledge of—"

"She mentioned documentation," Mercer continued. "Letters. Records. Notes. I assumed those would be here at the historical society, yes?"

"They might be," I said. "But she also said she wanted one more night with her notes before showing us anything. So maybe—"

Mercer's eyes sharpened. "They're at her home."

"Yes."

Mercer glanced toward the hall, as if she could see straight through the building to Chestnut Drive. "Has anyone secured her home?"

I hesitated. "I don't know. That would be . . . family, wouldn't it? Though I don't think she had any family—"

She cut me off again. "Or the executor of her estate."

"Do we know who that is?"

Mercer shook her head. "Not yet."

I absolutely did not want to be a part of this mess, but somehow I kept getting dragged into it. I put my foot down. "I have nothing to offer other than what I've already told everyone. I think it's best you talk with people in the know. I am not one of them."

Maybelline and the historical society were drowning in logistics. The sheriff was handling the investigation. Lawyers were circling. Everyone was waiting for an estate process that moved at the speed of molasses in an ice box.

Meanwhile, Virginia's house was just . . . sitting there.

"If there are documents supporting provenance," Mercer said, "they're valuable. If they're missing, it matters. Not only to ownership but to motive."

"Motive?"

She pursed her lips.

Of course motive. It was all connected. And I was intrigued, despite myself.

I pictured Virginia's calm face in her hallway that afternoon. The covered painting. The careful way she'd spoken—unsure, sentimental.

*One more night.*

Mercer's gaze held mine. "If you hear anything—anything at all—about her papers or correspondence, please let me know."

"Right," I said, because I didn't know what else to say.

"Thank you. I'll leave you to it, then," and she left the office.

She hadn't asked me to do anything improper. She hadn't even suggested it. But I felt the nudge anyway.

Not just from Mercer's urgency.

It was my own curiosity poking at me.

Virginia's house sat unguarded while people with briefcases and claims and tense backstories made plans. Ralph was still sick, but also defensive, and he'd listened to Virginia's late-night message without telling Sheriff Brooks about it at all.

I realized suddenly that I was alone in his office.

Ralph's desk was covered in papers—folders half-open, sticky notes, meeting agendas, donor lists. I leaned in just enough to scan without touching. My eyes snagged on a few familiar words—fundraiser, vendor, printing—then slid right past them, hunting for anything that might say Virginia.

Nothing jumped out.

I straightened, heart thumping.

But then I thought about that message. The one Ralph had admitted he heard. The one he'd been awfully cagey about.

I needed to make a call.

That was a perfectly normal thing to do in an office. I was a volunteer. I was part of the fundraiser machine. I could call Maybelline, ask what she needed next, act like a responsible citizen.

So I picked up the receiver.

My finger hovered for a second, then I went into voicemail like I'd done a hundred times at O'Malley's—they had the same ancient beige phone in their kitchen.

The automated voice chirped to life, cheerful as a cartoon.

“You have zero new messages. You have zero saved messages.”

I froze.

Zero.

Not one saved. Not one archived. Not even a “press one to replay.”

Just . . . nothing.

Maybe Ralph really had been half-delirious with the flu and erased it by accident.

Or on purpose.

Virginia Marks had called for a reason. And whatever she’d said wasn’t sitting there waiting to be heard anymore.

Gone, just like Virginia.

# Chapter Thirteen

I told myself I was going home. That was the plan.

Instead, my car drifted toward Chestnut Drive of its own accord.

Virginia's neighborhood was quiet, the yards neat, the shrubs clipped back for winter. A few early buds dotted the branches—stubborn little signs of life taking the risk that the cold would go away for good.

Virginia's house, however, looked exactly like what it was. Closed for business.

I could've driven on. I should've. Instead, I pulled up to the curb, put the car in park, and sat there for a moment, hands resting on the steering wheel. I stared at Virginia's front door like I expected her to appear and remind me that unannounced visits were a sign of poor upbringing.

Why was I here?

Virginia had led Trudy and me straight to her back room—study, library, storage room, whatever you wanted to call it. The curtains had been open then, sunlight pouring in. I could hear the antique clock ticking as we stood in that room. I remembered seeing a wide desk with neat stacks of papers and folders. I hadn't known her well at all, but I got the distinct sense that she was an orderly woman who did things the right way. No shortcuts, no sir.

Now I found myself out of my Jeep and circling toward the side yard, careful not to disturb her garden beds. That mattered.

There was a way to be curious in the South without being rude about it, and there's a way to be rude without meaning to. I was trying very hard to stay on the polite side of that line.

From the side window, the curtain hung slightly uneven.

And the lower sash sat raised a couple of inches.

That I knew hadn't been the case before.

Virginia wouldn't have cracked a window, not here in the mountains, still winter. Not when the air still had a bite to it.

I stepped closer, careful not to press against the glass.

Inside, the room no longer looked precise.

A file drawer sat pulled halfway out. Papers were scattered across the rug. The desk was nearly clear save for two other things I remembered: a small lamp with a fringed shade and a brass paperweight of a little girl and her dog.

The police had been through, of course. They would've opened drawers, moved items, taken photographs. But this didn't look like careful procedure. It looked like someone had been searching for something specific.

I noticed the easel was still there, looking naked without the sheet, which appeared to be gone along with the painting.

Had Virginia been the one to move it? Or had it been stolen?

I let my gaze drift along the window frame. The screen was slightly bent at one corner. Not torn or ripped out, but pressed inward . . . and then set back into place.

If someone had come in through that window, they weren't after jewelry or cash. They were after the painting—most likely—and the documentation that came with it.

Virginia's notes.

Letters.

Provenance.

Anything that told the truth of how that painting had landed in her hands.

I stood there too long, my mind flipping through every single thing I'd learned since Virginia had died. It took my breath away.

I slowly stepped back from the window, feeling guilty. I wasn't supposed to be here. Not like this. Not alone. Not peering into a dead woman's study like a nosy raccoon with a purse.

But I couldn't unsee it.

I walked back to my car the way my mother taught me to move in public: like I belonged, even if I didn't. I slid into the driver's seat, locked the doors, and sat there with my hands on the wheel. I realized I was shivering.

"Okay," I muttered. "Okay, Betty."

I didn't look at the house again. I started the engine and pulled away. But again, I didn't go home.

Because one thing was suddenly very clear:

If someone was hunting Virginia's papers, then whatever she knew was more dangerous than I'd realized.

And whether Harlan liked what I'd done or not . . . I was going to have to tell him what I'd seen.

# Chapter Fourteen

I made the call hands-free while I drove, staring straight ahead because if I looked anywhere else my brain might crack in half.

Harlan answered on the second ring. "Brooks."

"It's Betty," I said, my voice quivering.

"I have caller ID, you know." When I didn't hit him with a comeback, he said, "What's going on?"

"I need to talk to you. In person."

A pause. "Where are you?"

"In my Jeep," I admitted. "I'm . . . out. Driving."

"Driving where, exactly?"

"I'm headed, er . . . away from Chestnut Drive," I said. "I'm not there. I left. But I saw something, and I don't want to say it over the phone."

I grimaced, waiting for the reprimand. I could just picture him rolling his eyes and cursing me silently.

"Are you alone?" he asked.

"Yes."

"All right." He paused. "Listen to me. You're going to meet me at O'Malley's."

"Not the station?"

"I'm waiting for my lunch at the bar counter. I'll move to a booth near the back and ask Rhonda not to seat anyone near us," he said.

"O'Malley's," I repeated, and my chest loosened a fraction.

It was better than confessing my snoopiness to him in his office.

"You drive straight there. No detours. You walk in like you're coming for lunch, you hear me?"

"Yes," I said, stopping at a light.

"Good. I'll see you in a few."

He hung up.

I sat there until the light turned green, then put my blinker on and shook loose the tension in my neck and shoulders. I was a perfectly normal woman about to run an errand. Everything was fine. Right as rain.

---

O'Malley's was steady-busy when I walked in, the lunch crowd starting to filter in. I waved at Rhonda, who pointed to the far corner. My gaze shifted in that direction, and Harlan waved me over. I moved as normally as I could, but I still felt like all eyes were on me and my legs weighed a hundred pounds each.

Harlan had his big hands clasped on the table, a club soda off to the side. He didn't look relaxed, exactly, but he didn't look too awfully angry at me.

Before I could even sit, Hank Whitfield strolled by with that easy confidence of his—like every room existed partly for his enjoyment. He spotted me immediately, then noticed Harlan.

"Well now," he said, slowing just enough to be a nuisance. "If this ain't a sight."

"Hank," I warned.

He lifted both hands in surrender. "I was just about to say hello. You look... intense."

"I'm fine," I said automatically.

Hank's eyes flicked between me and Harlan—curious, but smart enough not to press. "All right then. Carry on." He gave a quick nod to Harlan, then kept walking toward a back booth like he hadn't just inserted himself into my nervous system.

I slid into the booth across from Harlan.

Rhonda appeared. "I know you're having a meeting, but real quick . . . Betty, you want coffee or something stronger?"

"Coffee," I said, though I craved a double bourbon, neat.

We waited until she brought the coffee, and I thanked her as she hurried off.

Harlan leaned forward slightly. "All right," he said. "Talk."

I wrapped both hands around the mug and stared straight into it like the answers might rise up with the steam.

"I went by Virginia's house," I said.

"I gathered."

"I know," I said quickly, looking up at him. "I know. But listen—I didn't go inside. I didn't touch anything."

He didn't blink. "Continue."

"The study window was cracked," I said. "That's where she brought Trudy and me to see the painting—only we didn't. Which you know already. So, anyway, the window was open, the screen was bent, and the curtains were parted. And I could see straight into the room."

I paused. Harlan didn't move. It was unnerving but effective, I had to admit.

I continued. "It was a mess. Not from the police, at least I don't think so. Someone was seriously looking for something specific."

"You see the painting?" he asked.

"No," I said. "The easel was there, but the room looked like a tornado had come through there. It was bad. And . . . sad."

He stayed still for a beat longer, then nodded once. "You did the right thing telling me."

That wasn't what I expected to hear.

"Thank—"

He cut in. "You don't go back there, you hear me?"

"I won't," I said, and this time I meant it. "I swear."

"Good." He took a slow breath. "Because I'm not wanting to see you hurt, Betty, as much as you irritate the heck out of me. I'll get someone over there right away to check things out."

Relief loosened something in my chest. "Thank you."

He studied me. "If you're feeling like you're about to do something you know you shouldn't, maybe call a friend. Call me, even. Before you do it."

I managed a tight smile. "You're asking a lot."

He didn't return the smile. "I'm telling you what keeps you alive."

That wiped the smile off my face. "You're absolutely right. But all in all, I do hope this helps. Maybe you can get finger-prints or—"

"Stop."

"Okay." And I took a sip of my coffee.

Rhonda brought his food, and for a few moments we just sat there in silence, the bar noise washing around us, normal life happening in the middle of not-normal things.

Harlan took the last bite of his burger, slid a few bills onto the table, and stood.

"I've got to get back to the station," he said. "Go home after this. I'm sure that was not the most pleasant experience you've ever had."

"I do feel like I need to decompress," I admitted.

"Then go do it. And thanks for telling me what was going on."

He headed for the door.

I watched him leave, my coffee cooling in front of me, when another bright idea popped into my head.

If there was ever a time to ask an old mountain man for more details about the Holloways and Halfords . . .

Tomorrow would be it.



# Chapter Fifteen

I wasn't so dimwitted as to not call Harlan and let him know that I wanted to talk to his uncle. Not snoop around anywhere. Just ask a few questions, and I promised to share anything important the moment I got back.

Surprisingly, he gave me the green light *and* Earl's cell phone number. I couldn't believe that man had a cell phone. I called it, but no one answered, and his voicemail box was full. I smiled at that. One way to keep the spammers at bay.

Up the mountain I went.

I wasn't sure what had changed from the time Harlan and I had visited to today, but the mud was plentiful. The logical guess would be the snow melt. I hadn't anticipated that. By the time I turned off the paved highway and started up the narrow mountain road toward Earl's cabin, I was already reconsidering the wisdom of my decision.

The road was downright ornery today.

The first stretch was rutted but passable. I eased the Jeep forward, tires slipping once or twice before catching again. Patches of thawed earth gleamed dark and slick amidst the lingering frost. I kept both hands steady on the wheel.

"Easy now," I murmured, as if the vehicle were a nervous horse. Worse, I'd never ridden a horse. Not once in all my Southern-lovin' years.

Halfway up the incline, the back tires spun. The Jeep fishtailed once, then settled crooked across the narrow track.

I pressed my lips together and shifted into reverse, backing down carefully a few feet. I tried again with less throttle.

The tires whined. The Jeep slid sideways and stopped.

"Good . . . ness," I murmured, rubbing my forehead. "This is a heckuva thing."

I sat for a moment, considering what to do now. I wasn't very close to Earl's cabin; at least I didn't think so. I looked at my phone. I could make a call for assistance. But that seemed like it would take way too much time that I didn't want to spend. *Think, Betty, think.* What had Salvy taught me about getting stuck in the mud? Not metaphorically, which happened often for me when writing screenplays; others called it writer's block. But actually getting stuck in the mud? What was the trick?

Heck if I knew.

I glanced around. No houses. No passing traffic. Just trees, damp ground, and silence.

Wiping a trickle of sweat from my brow, I tried once more. This time the back end sank. Not deep. But deep enough.

I shut off the engine and stepped out. The ground swallowed my left boot almost to the ankle. I pulled it free with a sucking sound that seemed to echo.

"Hello? Anyone out there," I called out, on the off chance someone was hiking somewhere nearby. My words echoed back at me. Or at least they seemed to.

Then I heard it.

The low, rolling baying of hound dogs carried through the trees. Dog and Girl. Maybe they'd come to my rescue. I suddenly wished I'd brought a couple of steaks with me.

I circled the Jeep, assessing. Sure enough, the rear tires were stuck and stuck good.

I reconsidered walking the rest of the way. Earl's place couldn't be more than a quarter mile ahead. I wasn't in the best of shape—yoga kept me busy, but it wasn't like I put a whole lotta effort into it. I was there for the social aspect.

The slow crunch of boots on gravel ...

I turned.

Earl appeared like an angel sent straight from heaven, and it was as if the trees parted and the ground solidified to allow safe passage. At his side were the hounds.

He walked with ease, hat pulled low, coat zipped to his chin, hands tucked into the pockets. Unhurried, as if stuck vehicles were simply another part of the season.

He stopped a few feet away and looked at the Jeep. Then at my boots.

"You made it this far," he said.

"Not quite far enough." I chuckled awkwardly.

He nodded once. "Road's soft today."

"I gathered."

He walked around the back of the vehicle, crouched slightly, and pressed his palm against the clay beside the tire. When he stood again, there was no change in his expression.

"Needs boards," he said.

"Boards," I repeated.

He didn't elaborate. He simply turned and walked back up the road toward his cabin.

I stood there for half a second, not sure what to do. Stay or go.

I followed him and the canine crew up the slope.

The cabin came into view around the bend. Smoke rose in a thin line from the chimney. Earl disappeared inside and returned moments later carrying two weathered planks.

He handed one to me without ceremony. “For behind the tires,” he said.

And down the slope we all went.

We worked in silence, easing the boards beneath the rubber. I slid around in the mud, but somehow managed to stay off my backside.

“Let’s give it a try now,” Earl said, wiping his hands on the seat of his pants.

I got behind the wheel, and he stepped back, lifting his hand.

The go signal, I presumed. I eased the Jeep forward. The tires caught. The vehicle lurched and rolled free.

I let out a long breath, feeling like I was about to pass out from relief. “You wanna ride?” I asked him through the open window.

But he’d already started walking up the slope, Dog and Girl pulling up the rear.

Moments later, I parked on the firmer ground near the cabin. Earl was washing his hands under a spigot near the cabin. I pulled out a couple of wet wipes from the glove box, cleaned up, then got out.

“You saved the day, Earl.”

“You were loud.”

I smiled. “I’ll try to be more graceful next time.”

He regarded me a moment, then gestured toward the cabin door. “Coffee.”

We stepped inside, and the warmth found me, snuggling me like a winter coat. I wanted to take off my boots and heat my toes by the fire, but I refrained. The man had probably had his fill of me today already.

He poured coffee into two mismatched mugs and set one before me. "You don't come up here for nothing," he said.

"No," I admitted, clearing my throat. I wrapped my hands around the mug, took a sip, then cleared my throat. "I have a question."

"Go on."

"Why would someone risk breaking in?" I asked. "For a painting that's already missing . . . or for whatever she wrote down about it?" I shook my head. "It feels like they were looking for something specific."

Earl didn't react immediately. He took a slow sip of his coffee and waited.

"Someone's been in her study," I continued. "Window cracked, screen bent, all the things. The room looked like it had been searched, and not by Harlan and his team."

Earl's eyes stayed steady on mine. "After she died," he said.

"Yes."

He took another sip. "Folks don't break in for nothing."

"No, they don't. And if she was keeping documentation, which I have to believe she was . . ."

"Then they didn't want it found," he said quietly.

I met his eyes. "That's what I'm afraid of. And that got me to thinking about how she'd come to own that painting at all."

He stood and crossed to the wall where several old maps were pinned beneath small brass tacks. They were not decorative pieces. They were working maps—creased at the folds, penciled notations in the margins, certain parcels outlined more than once.

He tapped a spot near the lower edge. "Halfords," he said, then tapped another spot close to it. "Holloways."

Setting my mug on the table, I moved closer to get a better view. "So that's where the properties are. Big pieces of land."

He went on as if he hadn't heard me. "Old papers makin' new trouble."

What did that mean? I thought about it for a beat or two. "Are you saying Virginia had some papers that would cause problems between the two families? Like, the painting isn't the main issue, or . . . ?"

"Painting's tied to more than the art," he said, his gaze glued to the map. "Land's never just dirt."

"Right," I said, hands on my hips, nodding like I knew what he was talking about. I felt like I was getting closer to some answers, though I didn't know in what way.

"So let's say Virginia was close to proving something," I said slowly, "and someone stole her notes . . ."

"Then they're scared," Earl finished for me.

"Scared of what?"

He didn't answer. Maybe he didn't know.

He moved back to the table and sat down, folding his hands loosely. "You drive careful going down," he said, my cue to leave.

I almost laughed. "You say that like I have options."

"Mud's worse on the way back."

"That's encouraging." I headed for the door and turned just before walking outside. "See you, Earl. Thanks for your time."

He regarded me a moment longer. "Don't go chasing paper alone."

I tilted my head. "I don't chase."

"Mm."

Which meant he didn't believe me.

Outside, the wind moved gently through the trees. I looked

at the path downward and it seemed to be mocking me. Despite Earl's words of caution, I figured going down was going to be a whole lot easier than coming up the mountain. At least I knew to be more careful now.

I glanced back once toward the cabin. Earl stood in the doorway, mug in hand. Dog and Girl were nowhere to be found.

He hadn't given me answers. He had given me context. I didn't know how to piece it all together, but I still felt like the trip had been worth its weight in mud.

I pulled myself up into the driver's seat and started the engine, doing a slow U-turn to face the way down. Then I proceeded, pressing the pedal then letting up, pressing, letting up . . . praying I'd make it to pavement sooner than later.

And my mind rolled with similar starts and stops. Virginia had wanted one more night with her painting, and I had thought it was maybe sentiment or making sure she had all her ducks in a row.

But what if it was, like Earl had hinted, something more than just the painting that had caused her to hesitate? Like she'd been worried the painting would cause some sort of stir . . . another family feud?

I made it to the main road without incident. But mud season, it seemed, had only just begun.

# Chapter Sixteen

By the time I returned from my walk along the lake, the sun had lifted high enough to make the water shimmer, as if inviting all the residents to come and play. The air carried that damp, mineral scent that always followed a thaw. Despite all that loveliness, I was uncomfortable—my stretchy pants seemed to want to suck the life out of me.

I stepped onto my porch just in time to see Nutty dart across the railing, tail flicking with proprietary confidence. He dropped something near the door, then scurried atop a gnome statue I'd purchased just recently from Serenity Garden Center.

"Honestly," I said, bending to retrieve the prize. "If this is another fishing hook, we're going to have a talk."

It wasn't. It was a small brass button, dulled with age. I turned it in my fingers, amused.

"You're building me a wardrobe, aren't you?"

Nutty chittered, then took off. He had more important things to deal with than me.

Inside, the front windowsill had become a quiet testament to squirrel devotion. Nutty's treasures included pebbles, a sliver of blue glass, a penny, two acorn caps, and, yes, a fishing hook. I placed the button amongst the others, then headed to the bathroom for a warm shower.

But I didn't make it that far. I was still smiling when the knock came at the door.

Maybelline Griggs stood on the porch looking composed but alert, like a woman holding several threads in one hand and hoping none of them snapped.

“I won’t keep you long,” she said. Before I could invite her in, she swept past me into my living room, eyes scanning my face the way Trudy did when she thought I was about to do something dumb. Or sneaky. “Actually, I need you at the Society.”

My smile faded. That shower and a mug of tea was feeling like a distant relative now. “Is this about the fundraiser or the Holloway art?”

Maybelline’s mouth tightened. “Both.”

Of course.

She lowered her voice, and I wondered who she thought might be listening. “The lawyers sent another letter. Ralph is . . . not helpful. And Laurel Halford has started asking questions in that sweet way people do when—” She bit her lip.

“When . . .?” I prompted.

“I guess when they’re trying to sound harmless but have something specific they want to know and they don’t want to come out and say it.”

“About what?” I asked, though I already had an inkling.

Maybelline’s gaze flicked to my windowsill treasures. She looked confused for a long second as she stared at them, then returned her gaze back to me. “About what we have. What we don’t have. And what Virginia might’ve told anyone before she died.”

A small chill slid through me. “So what do you need from me?”

“I need you to help me,” she said simply. “Help me stay focused on the fundraiser. Help me keep the historical society from falling apart. Ralph is downright useless. He's been in a tizzy about . . . well, pretty much everything. I'm in over my head. Can you come in for an hour? We're getting all the signage in order. And we need to decide on the wording for the plaques for the two Holloways that Joyce donated. If we're going to move forward with the fundraiser, we at least need to look like we know what we're doing."

That was Maybelline in a nutshell. Everything was a crisis lately. But I respected her for sticking to the task.

"All right," I said. "You go on ahead of me. You do not want me to miss my shower right now."

---

The historical society had that kind of buzzy vibe that usually preceded a big event. Well-meaning people moving too fast, papers shuffling, voices bouncing off the old walls. Someone was arguing near the coat rack about whether "Winter Heritage" sounded depressing.

Now that we were heading into springtime, I could see their point. Who wanted to talk about winter anymore?

I slipped past the ornate vases filled with pretty dried-flower bouquets and found Maybelline in the small gallery room.

The two Holloway paintings hung side by side under soft track lighting. Not officially "on display" yet, but this was the first time I'd really had a chance to see them up close and personal.

And they were gorgeous. Breathtaking. Each brushstroke had purpose; the colors blended like a dream. I couldn't take my eyes off them.

"They've been professionally cleaned," Maybelline said

softly. “We’ll have one of them velvet ropes to keep people from touching. And like I mentioned, we really need to finalize the wording on the plaques. Bill from Trophies Plus is toe-tapping, waiting for us to get the information to him. What do you think?”

I stepped a wee bit closer, hands behind my back. “What a treat these are, is what I think.”

The first painting was soft winter light and stillness—bare trees, snow crusted on stone, a fence line leading your eye toward a farmhouse tucked back in the distance. The second was different. Same season, same hand, but the composition shifted. More open land, more sky, and it reminded me how small a big house really was compared to the world around it.

Then my attention snagged on . . . something. I narrowed my eyes to bring it more into focus.

The fence line on the first painting. Not the fence itself, but the direction the fence ran. Behind the fence, a low stone wall veered slightly in another direction. I would have expected it to follow the fence line.

“Hmm. That’s odd.”

I could feel Maybelline’s eyes on me. “What? Is there a problem?” Then she looked at the paintings. “Oh, my soul . . . did the conservator mess something up when he cleaned these?”

“I don’t know,” I admitted. “It’s just . . . he’s so consistent and detailed in every single way. But that stone wall and the fence don’t go in the same direction. In fact . . .”

“What? Spit it out, Betty.”

“That wall is not as clear as the rest of the paintings. Almost like a ghost wall. Not really there.” I stepped back. “You see what I’m saying?”

She leaned forward so far I was afraid she'd fall right into the display. "Umm, not really."

Maybe I needed my readers, which were in my purse. I shrugged it off and said, "Well, I think they're quite lovely."

But Maybelline stayed frozen in her precarious stance, eyeballing the painting. "You mean the fence and the wall."

Wasn't that what I just said? "Uhh-huhh." I nodded slowly.

"Look harder."

She tilted a wee bit forward, and I couldn't help it. I grabbed her arm. "Maybe not that hard."

She snapped out of her trance. "I really don't see anything that strange. Maybe if we had the middle painting, it would all make more sense. But wow, they are real lookers, aren't they?"

But I had snagged on her remark about the middle painting completing the picture. The missing third of the set.

"A series," I murmured as I stared at the duo. "Maybelline, these paintings are not standalones. You're right—they go together, and the middle painting would complete a bigger picture."

I glanced at her. She was studying me like I was wearing clown makeup. "Um, yeah?"

She wasn't buying what I was selling. Or maybe more accurately, she couldn't even see my point. I decided to let it go. I did have a tendency to make something out of nothing. "Well, I'm just saying . . . it would be nice to, uh, see the whole thing."

Maybelline cleared her throat and dragged me to a table. "Let's get crackin'. I need you to go over this information, what we know about the history of the paintings, and write something snappy."

"Snappy?"

"Exactly," she said and flew off to peck at someone else.

I toyed with the papers in front of me, scanning the highlights. It wouldn't take me long to write something, but no matter what my words would be, they wouldn't be enough. Because we didn't have the one picture . . . which would give us the whole picture. And that seemed mightily important.

For more reasons than one.

Earl had given me plenty to think about the day before. And I knew I wasn't completely off my rocker about that stone wall. Or how the fence and the wall seemed to part ways, when I would have expected them to follow each other.

And if the missing painting showed the middle stretch—whatever Holloway put there—then maybe the Winter Garden series wasn't just a set of pretty winter scenes.

Maybe it was a record.

And if it was a record—an honest one—then someone had a very good reason to keep the third piece hidden.

# Chapter Seventeen

Yoga was supposed to be calming.

Yoga was supposed to be breath and balance and letting go.

Today, it was a room full of women talking about the death of Virginia Marks. And her missing painting. Typical Bluejay Ridge vine of whispers. Of which I was wholly a part.

The studio had once been a feed barn, now converted into a light, airy space with tall windows and lots of bamboo and wicker decor. Whenever I was here, I felt like I had a higher purpose, something more than flexibility and trying to keep my hips from going out on me. No, it was also a social event, a place where good people shared good gossip, the kind that kept the gears cranking and laughter flowing.

A slow instrumental track played in the background, and I laid my mat down, near the front but off to the side. I preferred not to be setting an example for the rest of the class.

Jolene swept in wearing matching leggings, shoes, and top, looking like she belonged in a catalog called *Lean and Lucky*. "Hey, Tater Tater," she teased, then whipped out her mat with a flourish.

I lobbed one back at her. "Your earrings don't match."

Her mouth formed an O as she touched her ears. "Darn it."

Trudy arrived a minute later with her cane and a red bandana fashioned as a headband that wrapped around her forehead, like she was a runner from the 1970s. Or a brick layer.

"You're late," I said.

She spread her mat on the other side of me. "I'm not late. I'm precisely on time."

Our instructor, the gorgeous Jack Harmon, clapped his hands gently, as if he were afraid to startle us into panic, and the room settled. We moved through warmups, slow stretches, breath work. My body knew the routine even if my brain refused to participate. I was itching to tell Trudy and Jolene the latest.

We shifted into warrior pose—my all-time favorite because I had thighs of steel, even if they were a little squatty. And it made me feel powerful, like a true soldier of life. As I held the stance, my mind slid right back to Virginia's study window. Cracked open, screen bent, the room inside looking like a tornado had blown through.

I wobbled.

Without turning her head, Jolene whispered, "If you fall, I'm laughing."

I was more determined than ever to stay upright. I even held the pose a little longer than necessary, giving Jolene the High Brow.

She snorted out a giggle, and suddenly all eyes were on us.

Jack said, "Ladies . . ." and Jolene laughed harder.

After class, the room filled with the familiar sounds of yoga people opening water bottles, rolling up mats, and complaining about hamstrings. The normalness was comforting.

Trudy tapped her cane once against the floor. "All right. Talk."

"Trudy," I said, rolling my mat into a tight tube, "not here."

"Since when?" She screwed up her face like she'd just caught a whiff of roadkill. "'Round here, privacy is a myth."

Jolene drifted over like a shark who'd smelled blood. "Yes. Talk."

I pressed my lips together. "Fine. But brief."

"Brief," Jolene repeated.

I kept my voice low. "I saw Uncle Earl again the day before yesterday." I filled them in on that visit and how he had told me a whole lot of nothing that felt like a Big Something. "And I went to the historical society yesterday. Saw the two Holloways up close."

Trudy's eyes sharpened. "And?"

"And they're gorgeous," I admitted. "But they don't feel like standalones. They feel like parts of a whole."

Jolene made a thoughtful noise. "Like a trilogy."

"A book series," Trudy added.

"Exactly," I said. "And on the first painting, there's a stone wall and a fence line, but they go off in different directions. Or at least it looks like they do. And it's not by much, but it is curious."

Trudy's gaze shifted, unfocused for a second, like she was looking at something far away. "Stone wall," she repeated.

"Yeah. Oh, and it's faint. Almost like it's not really there." I hesitated. "Maybelline said something interesting too."

Jolene leaned in. "Oh, good. I love interesting."

"Laurel Halford has been asking questions," I said.

Trudy snorted. "About what?"

I frowned. I didn't know. I hadn't even thought to ask. "I presume about the missing painting. I honestly am not sure."

Trudy tapped my leg with her cane. "That would have been a good—"

"Yes, I know. A good question to ask. But anyway, I started

thinking. It seems like the middle painting isn't just missing. It's important in another way."

Trudy went still. Just for a beat.

Then she shook it off. "Of course it's important. It's valuable. People lose their minds over valuable things."

"Right," I said. "But I don't think it's just money."

Jolene's eyes narrowed. "What else would it be?"

I started to answer, but Trudy's face tightened again—another little flicker.

"Trudy?" I asked, worried she might be having small seizures or something. "Are you okay?"

She blinked. "What?"

"You keep freezing up and staring off into the distance." So, Jolene had noticed it too. She continued. "It's like your brain is pretending it doesn't know something it definitely knows."

Trudy made a face. "It is not."

"It is so," Jolene insisted.

"I have to admit, I saw it too," I added.

Trudy's jaw worked. "It's . . . nothing. Probably."

"It's not nothing," I said, softer now. "If you remember something, please tell us."

"We're your tribe. You can trust us," Jolene said, placing an arm around the older woman.

Trudy hesitated, then sighed like she hated all of us.

"I keep thinking about Virginia's house," she said. "Not any specific thing in it, but the way she ran that place. She didn't always do it herself. She had help sometimes."

"Help," Jolene repeated, and her eyebrows jumped.

"There was a woman," Trudy went on. "Years back. A good'un. Worked for folks. Housekeeping. Cooking. That kind of thing."

My skin prickled. “For Virginia?”

Trudy shook her head. “Not just Virginia. She worked all around town. But still . . .”

Jolene’s mouth twisted, like she was trying to pull a name from the air. “She had one of those hyphen names.”

Trudy’s eyes narrowed, looking deep in thought. “No, I don’t think so.”

“Not a hyphen name,” Jolene corrected. “But two names, maybe. Old-fashioned.” She started snapping her fingers, as if that would help her remember.

My heart beat a little faster. In my book, this was a huge revelation.

Trudy rubbed her forehead. “I can’t place it. I just know Virginia wasn’t as alone as people made her out to be. Somebody helped her. Somebody knew her routines.”

“And somebody might’ve known what she had, like that painting,” I said, the words slipping out before I could stop them.

Trudy’s gaze locked on mine. “Exactly.”

I was about to start brainstorming names when my phone buzzed from my gym bag.

I pulled it out and looked at the caller ID. “It’s Harlan.”

All three of us froze like we’d been caught doing something we shouldn’t have been doing.

I stepped a few feet away, but both women followed me just the same.

“Harlan,” I said.

“Betty,” he replied. “You got a second?”

“For you, Harlan, always.” I chuckled.

He only cleared his throat. That told me everything.

“Oh no,” I said. “What’s wrong?”

"It's about Virginia's house," he said. "We checked it."

My throat tightened. "And?"

"It was a break-in, for sure. Someone was in there after we'd processed and cleared the house. After Virginia died."

My stomach dropped. "So it wasn't—"

"No," he said, firm. "It definitely wasn't us. It wasn't a case of sloppy procedure. Somebody came back for something. You did right by telling me. It brings this whole investigation into another level."

I stared at the studio wall, at a framed quote about peace that seemed to be mocking me.

"What did they take?" I asked.

"That's the problem," he said. "Hard to tell what's missing in a house like that unless you know what was there."

I thought of the empty easel. The stripped desk. The scattered papers.

"The study, though," I said. "They were focused on the study, right?"

"Mostly, but not exclusively. Other parts of the house looked searched. Beyond what we would have done."

My grip tightened on the phone. "Did you get prints?"

"A few partials," he said. "Nothing clean yet. But we did get something else."

My stomach tightened. "What?"

"A boot print in the mud under the study window," he said. "Work boot tread. Partial, but clear enough to tell it's around a size ten."

I swallowed. "That could be anybody."

"Exactly," he said. "But it tells me this wasn't some kid in sneakers. And here's what matters more: they weren't stealing. Jewelry wasn't touched, or at least it didn't look like it. There was plenty there worth taking. No electronics missing. They went through drawers and papers and cabinets like they were hunting for one specific thing."

My mind snapped straight to Virginia's covered easel. "The painting."

"Or whatever she wrote down about it," he said. "Either way, it wasn't a random burglary type of break-in." A pause. "Betty, I need you to hear me."

"I'm listening."

"You stay away from that house," he said. "And if you remember anything Virginia said about notes, correspondence, who she trusted—anything—tell me. Don't go chasing it. We've moved into serious trouble territory."

It wasn't like him to be so dramatic. "I have been up front with you, and I will continue to do so. In fact . . ." And I shared my conversation with Earl and what I saw at the historical society, in the paintings.

He grunted, then a long pause. "More pieces of the puzzle. Good work, Betty. It's slowly starting to come together."

"It is? How?"

The call ended.

I stood there for a moment longer than necessary, phone still pressed to my ear even though the line was dead.

When I turned around, Jolene and Trudy were watching me like I'd just come back from war.

"Well?" Jolene asked.

I swallowed. "Harlan confirmed Virginia's home had been broken into after she died. And he found a boot print under the study window. Size ten."

"It's what we'd expected him to say—that the home had been broken into," Trudy pointed out.

"True, but it wasn't a burglary. It was more purposeful."

"So," Jolene said, taking a wider stance and crossing her arms, "somebody wanted something very specific that Virginia had."

Trudy nodded once. "The painting, something about the painting, or both."

"Here's the thing," I said. "Harlan claims this case has now become more dangerous . . . for everyone involved. At least he thinks so."

"You're involved," Trudy said.

Jolene's eyes went big. "Mercy," she said.

*Took the word right out of my mouth.*

I thought of that nameless woman Trudy almost remembered—helping around Virginia's house, knowing routines, knowing where things were kept. And I thought of that size ten boot print. The break-in looking nothing like a good ol' burglary.

The story Virginia had been trying to tell us—whether with paint or paper—was more perilous than any of us had wanted to believe.

# Chapter Eighteen

By that afternoon, my mind was still stuck in warrior pose. But I felt helpless to do anything to move the investigation forward. We were reacting instead of acting, and I wanted to stop greasing the pan and start cooking the meal, so to speak.

I stood in my kitchen eating a Southern delicacy, pear salad—a canned pear half on lettuce with a dollop of mayo and a good sprinkle of shredded cheddar. I stared out the window while I ate, like the answer to a murder might wander across my yard wearing a name tag.

My phone buzzed.

Trudy.

"Hey," I answered.

"Where are you?" she asked, as if I might be in a hot air balloon over Tennessee.

"At home."

"Good. Stay there. I'm coming by."

She must have been sitting in my driveway when she called because it wasn't sixty seconds before she came a-knockin'. Though she didn't knock.

She burst through the door, shouting my name, and found me in the kitchen, rinsing dishes.

She looked wild. Wilder than I'd ever seen her.

My hopes shot straight through the ceiling. "Don't tell me."

She smirked. "Yup."

"You remembered."

"I sure did." She tapped the side of her head. "I still got it."

Wiping my hands on a dish towel, I slid into a chair and patted the table, urging her to do the same. "Do tell."

Her energy immediately changed. She sighed and her shoulders slumped.

"I hate this," she muttered, taking off her blazer and draping it over the back of the chair opposite me. But she didn't sit.

"You hate what—remembering?"

"No, no. I don't like dredging people up like they're evidence."

"Pfft. Since when? Besides, I'm not trying to dredge," I said. "I'm trying to understand who knew Virginia. Who was close. Who might've had access."

Trudy's mouth tightened. She nodded once, slow. "All right."

She walked to the windowsill and looked out over the backyard. "You got a thing for gnomes?"

I had the one on the porch, and a plethora scattered around the back. "They're like family. I'm lonely and whimsical," I deadpanned. "Stay on task."

Trudy snorted and took a seat. "It came to me in pieces after class. The name. The face. The way she'd talk. I called Jolene, and she remembered too."

My skin prickled. "Her name?"

Trudy lifted her chin. "Ruby Pearl."

Something in my chest shifted—like a latch clicking.

"Ruby Pearl," I repeated.

"Yep," Trudy said. "Ruby Pearl McCallister."

"McCallister," I echoed again, letting it settle. It sounded right. It sounded like a name that had been in Bluejay Ridge longer than any of us.

Jolene would have squealed. I did not squeal, but I wanted to.

"Does Jolene know?"

"People called her Mama though. Because she acted like one," Trudy said, voice softer now. "Not in a babying way. But she was there for people. Fed you when you were broke. Folded your laundry when you were sick. Showed up with dessert for no good reason."

I leaned against the counter. "And this woman worked for Virginia."

"Off and on," Trudy said. "When Virginia needed help, it was Ruby Pearl she called. Sometimes she didn't even have to call. Ruby Pearl sometimes just knew when you needed her."

"Was she family to Virginia?" I asked.

"Not blood. But people like Ruby Pearl tend to get woven into families. Especially up here."

I nodded slowly, mind turning. "And you said she worked all around town."

"She did," Trudy confirmed. "Half the old families had Ruby Pearl in their house at some point. Cleaning. Cooking. Checking on an elderly aunt. Sitting with somebody who didn't want to be alone."

She got up, opened the fridge, and poured herself some iced tea—sweet.

"So," I said carefully, "if anyone knew Virginia's routines—"

"Ruby Pearl would've," Trudy finished. "More than anyone, really. But that doesn't mean she'd hurt her. Don't you even start with that bullhockey."

"I'm not," I said quickly, realizing from Trudy's reaction that Ruby Pearl must still be alive. "I'm not saying she did anything. I'm saying she might be a big part of Virginia's story, including her, uh, afterlife. That's all."

Trudy's eyes narrowed. "Good. Because Ruby Pearl may have had a sharp tongue, but she wasn't the kind of woman who did harm."

"Sharp tongue I can handle," I said. "Where is she now?"

Trudy hesitated.

That was the first real pause.

"She passed," Trudy said quietly.

"Oh," I breathed, surprised at the little sting that came with it. My presumption had been wrong. "I'm sorry."

Trudy nodded once. "Years ago. Not recent."

So no direct interview would be in the cards. I supposed that would have been too easy.

"But," Trudy added, and her eyes sharpened again, "Ruby Pearl had a daughter. And a granddaughter. And if anybody in this town knows what Ruby Pearl knew, it'll be those women."

My pulse picked up. "Names?"

Trudy waved a hand. "Now you're doing it again."

"Doing what?"

"Turning people into a list," she said. Then she sighed. "Her daughter is Celeste. Lives over near the old mill road. The granddaughter—Kendra—works at Millie's Bakery sometimes when she isn't picking up shifts at that new boutique on Main."

"Celeste," I repeated. "Kendra. I think I've met her."

Trudy nodded. "And before you go barreling over there—"

"I wasn't—"

"Yes, you were," she snapped, then softened just a notch. "Just . . . be respectful. Ruby Pearl's been gone a long time. Folks don't like feeling used."

"I won't use them," I said. "I'll ask."

Trudy studied me for a moment, then reached into her jacket pocket and pulled out a small slip of paper. She handed it to me.

It was an address.

"And this?" I asked.

"Virginia's," Trudy said. "Not her house—and don't you go there. Her *storage unit.*"

My head snapped up. "Virginia had a storage unit?"

Trudy nodded, lips pressed together. "I forgot about it until this morning. Virginia rented one out by the highway. Been paying on it forever. I only remembered because I got stuck behind her once when she was turning in there."

A cold thrill slid through me.

"And who else knows?" I asked.

"Probably Maybelline," Trudy said. "Maybe Ralph. I don't know. Virginia didn't announce her business."

My mind raced, and I had the urge to grab my folio and write it all down. I didn't carry it around like I used to.

A missing painting.

Missing notes.

A break-in.

A beloved housekeeper with kin still in town.

And now a storage unit.

Trudy held up a finger. "Betty. Before your brain takes off, tell Harlan."

"I will," I said, though my voice came out too quick. "Why didn't you?"

"Not sure, to be honest. Just promise me you'll tell him."

"I promise," I said, and I meant it.

Trudy nodded, seemingly satisfied. Then she glanced at my windowsill again, and I heard a sound and turned that way too. It was Nutty, looking impatient.

"Probably wants some peanuts," I said, rising to grab a handful out of the pantry.

"I swear to God, if that squirrel brings you a wedding ring..."

"I'll accept it," I said. "Times are tough."

Trudy huffed a laugh, and for a second, the world felt normal again.

And if Virginia Marks had trusted anyone—really trusted them—with something she wasn't sure she should bring into the light...

It wouldn't have been a lawyer or a board member.

It would have been the woman who could take care of a secret the way she cared for others and their homes. Ruby "Mama" Pearl McCallister.

I stared down at the address in my hand. I knew exactly what I had to do next.

Tell Harlan.

Have a talk with Celeste, maybe Kendra.

Because if Ruby Pearl was the thread, then her family was where the knot might finally start to loosen.

# Chapter Nineteen

I did what Trudy told me to do. I called Harlan first. After all, I could respect a boundary or two.

He answered on the second ring. "Brooks."

"It's Betty," I said, and before he could get clever, I added, "I have something useful, and I'm trying very hard to do this the right way."

A beat of silence. Then, "Go on." Just like his Uncle Earl.

"Trudy remembered someone who used to help Virginia," I said. "A housekeeper. Ruby Pearl McCallister. Folks called her Mama."

Harlan didn't respond right away, and I pictured him pinching the bridge of his nose the way he did when I made his life harder.

Instead, he said, "I remember that name."

"Yup. Ruby Pearl's been gone a while, but her daughter is still here. Celeste. We need to talk to her. Or I could . . . on your behalf. You could deputize me."

"Not going to happen. But I also don't have to give you permission to talk to someone."

Well, this was new.

"But you listen to me," he continued. "You don't accuse anybody. You don't go poking around on private property. You ask questions like a decent human being, and if you learn something that matters, you call me."

"That I can do," I said, doing a weird sort of jig.

"And," he added, "you don't go alone."

I opened my mouth, then closed it again.

"Trudy can come," he said, as if he could read my argument before I made it. "Or Jolene. Or both. But not you by yourself. I'll be available in a few hours, if you can hold your horses until then."

"I won't go alone," I said, not wanting to wait for him.

He made a sound that might have been agreement. Or a warning.

"Call me when you're done," he said.

And the line went dead.

He really needed to improve his social skills.

—

I called Trudy, and she insisted on riding with me.

"This is not an interrogation," she said as we pulled onto the road. "This is a conversation with a family that's been through enough."

"I know that," I said.

"You say that," she replied, "and then you get your detective eyes."

"I do not have detective eyes."

Trudy made a noise. "You got eyes like a bloodhound homing in on an injured bird."

I didn't argue. Mostly because it was accurate.

Celeste McCallister lived out past the old mill road, in a small white house with a porch swing and wind chimes that I recognized from Serenity Garden Center. I had one of them on my own front porch. The yard was tidy, but not manicured—daffodils coming up in clusters, an azalea bush that looked ready to burst.

Trudy knocked, then stepped back with her hands folded like she was about to meet the pastor.

The door opened, and a woman in her late fifties stood there wearing a faded sweatshirt. Her expression was blank, bland, blah . . . I got the immediate impression she didn't suffer fools and didn't have time for nonsense.

Her eyes went straight to Trudy.

"Well," she said, "if it isn't Trudy Carter."

Trudy lifted her chin. "Celeste."

I cleared my throat. "Hi. I'm Betty Benino."

Celeste's gaze slid to me, quick and assessing. "I know who you are," she said. "Everybody does."

That was both comforting and uncomfortable at the same time.

Trudy spoke in a tone I'd never heard her use before—gentle and sweet. It gave me the creeps a little. Like a smiling evil clown. "We're sorry to bother you. Truly. But something came up, and we thought you might be able to help."

Celeste's mouth formed a straight line. She didn't invite us in right away. She looked past us, down the drive, to the left and to the right, like she was checking for suspicious activity.

Then she stepped back. "Come on."

The house smelled like lemon cleaner and cinnamon. It was a homey home. Not fancy or staged. The kind of home that had been lived in, hard and true.

We sat at a small kitchen table. Celeste didn't offer coffee. That was fine. I didn't trust myself with hot liquid anyway.

"What is this about?" Celeste asked, folding her arms.

Trudy didn't dance around it. "Virginia Marks."

Celeste's eyes flickered. Just once. "What about her?"

"She's dead," Trudy said softly.

Celeste's face didn't change, but something in her went still, like a door closing.

"I heard," she said. "Sheriff came by. Asked a few questions."

My pulse jumped. "He did?"

Celeste's eyes snapped to mine. "Yes, ma'am. He did. But before we could get into much, he got called out mid-conversation. He barely stayed five minutes. Y'all just missed him."

*That little stinker . . . he beat me to it.*

Trudy shot me a look. I shrugged.

I adjusted in my chair. "I'm sorry," I said, meaning it. "We're not here to cause problems. We're just trying to understand who knew Virginia. Who might've been close."

Celeste's mouth pulled tight. "Virginia wasn't close to anybody."

Trudy leaned forward. "She was close to your mother."

Celeste's eyes narrowed. "Don't you bring Mama into this."

Trudy didn't flinch. "We think she might have known things. About Virginia."

Silence settled over the table, heavy as a quilt.

Celeste turned her head slightly, staring at the window above the sink. For a moment, I thought she might tell us to leave.

Instead, she exhaled. "Sheriff said the same thing. Yes, Mama helped Virginia," she said finally. "Off and on. They were close, yes."

I kept my voice careful. "Did she ever mention anything about a painting?"

Celeste's gaze came back to me, sharp now. "What kind of painting?"

"A Holloway," I said. "Part of the Winter Garden series."

Celeste's face went blank. Then her lips turned downward, and she shook her head.

Trudy watched her closely. "Celeste . . ."

Celeste stood up so fast her chair scraped the floor. "Y'all need to go."

My heart dropped. "No, please. We're not accusing your mother of anything. We're trying to understand how Virginia ended up with something so valuable it might've gotten her killed. That had people showing up with legal letters and boot prints in the mud."

Celeste froze.

"Boot prints?" she repeated quietly.

I instantly regretted saying it. Trudy's eyes flashed at me.

Celeste looked between us, then back toward the hallway, like she was deciding whether to trust us or protect herself.

Finally, she walked into the next room and returned with an old shoebox.

She set it on the table like it weighed a hundred pounds.

"This was Mama's," she said. "I keep it because . . . well, because it's hers."

Inside were small things: a folded handkerchief, a worn photograph of Ruby Pearl smiling beside a Christmas tree, a few pressed flowers wrapped in wax paper, and a battered little notebook with a rubber band around it.

Celeste touched the notebook like it might bite. "Mama wrote down stuff about her jobs," she said. "Not everything. But enough. Addresses. Names. Who liked what kind of pie. Who tipped. Who didn't."

Trudy's face softened. "That sounds like Ruby Pearl."

Celeste shot her a look. "What do you know about her?"

"I hardly knew her," Trudy said.

"Right. You hardly knew her. So let me finish."

One tough cookie. I'd never seen Trudy dial it back because someone told her to. But she sat back in her chair and got quiet. Me? I didn't touch anything. I didn't even lean in too hard. I just waited.

Celeste flipped the notebook open, revealing thick, yellowed paper. Ruby Pearl's handwriting was neat and precise, like the woman herself, I imagined. She turned a few pages, then stopped.

Her finger tapped a line.

*Marks, V. – Chestnut Drive – Fridays*

Then her finger slid lower.

*Holloway place – back room – cover it*

My breath caught.

Celeste's eyes lifted to mine, and there was something almost angry there—like she'd carried this alone longer than she wanted to.

"Mama didn't steal anything," she said, like she could read my thoughts. "She was asked to get that painting out of a house where it didn't feel safe anymore. Folks were fighting. The wrong people were sniffing around."

Trudy went still beside me.

Celeste swallowed hard. "Mama brought it to Virginia because Virginia was discreet. Because Mama believed if truth was going to survive, it needed a reliable keeper."

My throat tightened. "So Virginia . . ."

"Was protecting it," Celeste said.

Celeste reached into the shoebox again and pulled out a paperback book with a cracked spine—some old romance novel with a shirtless man on the cover, the kind you found at yard sales and in your nightstand.

She opened it and slid out a folded note. She held it out to Trudy, not to me.

Trudy unfolded it carefully, her expression changing as she read. Then she handed it to me. The handwriting was the same as the notebook—clean, firm, no wasted strokes.

*Virginia,*

*This one isn't just pretty. It's old business. Keep it covered. Keep it quiet. If anybody comes asking, you don't know anything about it. Not a word. Not a word until you know the time is right. You'll know.*

*— Ruby Pearl*

I stared at the note until the words blurred. The ink looked off. Fainter, a little smudged at the edges. Not the original. The kind of copy you made with carbon paper. I wondered where the real copy was, if Virginia still had it. Or if had been lost to time.

Then my mind went to a hard truth: Virginia had been given this weighty responsibility without ever asking for it. She'd been close to lifting her burdens.

And now she was dead.

Celeste watched my face. "Mama kept records of everything. She once told me if anyone ever started asking about that painting, it meant trouble was coming back around. I never thought much about it."

Trudy's voice came out soft. "Seems she was right."

"Mama died the same year she gave it to Virginia. Like she knew her end was near."

"She was sick?" I asked.

Celeste nodded and pressed her fingers to her lips, clearly getting choked up. "She was an amazing woman."

My fingers tightened around the note. The middle painting hadn't just wandered into Virginia's life. It had been placed there. Virginia was its guardian, just like Ruby Pearl had been.

And if someone broke into Virginia's house after she was murdered . . . searched around like they knew exactly what to look for . . .

Then Ruby Pearl had been right.

And now the trouble wasn't coming. It was already here.

I forced myself to breathe. "Thank you," I said. "I know this isn't easy."

Her eyes flashed. "Just don't turn Mama into a suspect."

"She's not," I said. "And I won't."

Trudy reached across the table and placed her hand over Celeste's for the briefest moment, then pulled away. She stood. "We should go now."

As we walked to my Jeep, Trudy leaned in close. "You calling Harlan?"

"Well, he probably knows some of this already. Yes, I'm calling him."

"And you're going to tell him everything we found out, including that storage unit, right?"

"Yes, yes," I said, waving her off.

We climbed into the Jeep, and we traveled down the old mill road in silence.

I loved a good mystery. But I didn't love the part where the mystery started loving me back.

# Chapter Twenty

By the time I got back to town, my nerves felt like they'd been wrung out and slapped across a clothesline.

Trudy rode in silence beside me, staring out the window like she was watching the world for signs of trouble. Which . . . fair. If trouble wanted to show its face, Bluejay Ridge had never been shy about giving it a stage.

When we neared the mouth of the Lake Pointe loop, she finally spoke. "Call Harlan."

"I will," I promised.

"You call him now." And she jabbed a finger at me, her big hand hiding most of her face.

"Calm down, calm down. I'll do it right now." I pulled into the Chapel of Hope parking lot, pulled out my phone, and dialed.

Trudy folded her arms and sat there like a chaperone.

When he answered, I said, "Before you say anything, I did exactly what you told me to do."

A pause. "That's a first."

It was true—it was a first for me. Maybe I was growing up . . . *Nah. Just a fluke.* "Celeste had a notebook," I said. "It belonged to her mother, Ruby Pearl. It mentions Virginia and a 'Holloway place.' And there was a note Ruby wrote to Virginia about the painting, telling her to keep it covered, keep it quiet."

Silence on the line.

He was in thinking mode. I waited.

Finally he said, "You have the note?"

"No. Celeste does. But Trudy and I read it. We can tell you word for word."

"All right," he said. "I need to get by there again, anyway. Had to leave on an urgent call when I stopped in the first time."

"Celeste will be so happy to see you," Trudy muttered under her breath with a pocket full of sarcasm.

Harlan ignored her. "Anything else?"

I hesitated. "Trudy remembered something. Virginia had a storage unit."

On the other end, I heard a slight change in his breathing.

"Where?" he asked.

"Out by the highway. Trudy says she got stuck behind Virginia turning in there once. She remembered it this morning. She gave me the address."

"Don't go near it," he said immediately.

*Darn it.* "Okay, fine." I blew out a loud breath, almost a raspberry, to make sure he knew I was displeased. "But it's my clue."

"While I appreciate this information, it's my investigation. You're doing your civilian duty to share what you know. Not because you're a detective."

"I should be," I muttered, then louder I said, "I understand."

A beat. Then, "Good. You did good. Go home."

When we hung up, I turned to Trudy. "Happy?"

She smiled like the Grinch. "Indeed."

I pulled back onto the road and dropped Trudy at her door, thinking I might give Hank a call. We needed to move our cocktail hour up a few days.

Time for a little Southern Comfort. Take that however you wish.

Unfortunately, cocktail hour didn't happen. I didn't even make it home.

Maybelline called before I'd even pulled into my driveway.

"Betty," she said, breathless. "Where are you?"

"I'm almost home," I said. "Why?"

"They're here."

"Who's here?" I asked, though I already knew the shape of the answer.

Maybelline lowered her voice like the walls might repeat her. "The Halfords."

"Laurel and Beau? They're historical society members. Is that so unusual?"

"Yes," she hissed. "Because they've got that Atlanta lawyer with them. The tall one. They're in the gallery room, and Ralph is in his office pretending to be dead."

"I'll be there in ten," I said, already turning my wheel.

"Bless you," Maybelline breathed, and hung up.

---

I found Maybelline near the front desk, clutching her clipboard like it was a life raft.

"Where's Ralph?" I whispered.

Maybelline jerked her chin down the hall. "Still in his office. Door shut. Lights off. Like a possum."

"Lovely," I said.

She grabbed my arm. "Just be normal."

"I'm the picture of normal." I gave her the High Brow.

She shot back a look of her own. "Betty. Be *boring*."

That was a tall order. I was no actress.

In the gallery room, Laurel Halford stood with her arms crossed, frowning at the two Holloway paintings. I got the feeling she was a no-nonsense sort of person. And I respected that. As long as she didn't interfere with me doing what I needed to do, whatever that may be.

And she was elegant in that old-money way—cream coat, perfectly coiffed updo, and pearls of all things. Her smile turned on the moment she saw me, sweet as syrup and just as sticky.

"Ms. Benino," she said. "How nice."

"Good to see you again." We'd never spoken, but we'd seen each other at meetings.

Beside her was younger brother Beau, his hairline looking for a way out back. He too was put-together with fine clothing and shoes. He meandered around the small space, looking around with a childlike curiosity. Eyes big, a pleasant smile, hands in pockets.

When he noticed me, he gave a small nod and offered one hand. "I should have introduced myself long ago," he said quietly. "Wonderful to meet you."

"The pleasure is all mine, I'm sure," I said, because I could be high-society when I needed to be.

And to the side of the gallery entranceway was Mark Delaney, the lawyer, holding a thin folder like it was a lunch menu.

"Well, this is perfect timing," Maybelline said brightly, loud enough for the whole room. "Laurel was just asking about the exhibit plaques, Betty."

Laurel's smile did not falter. "I was actually asking about the third painting."

Of course she was. But really . . . who wasn't? Still, her question got my ire up. She knew good and well the painting was missing and that no one knew what had happened to it.

"I wish we had more information about where it might be," I said evenly. "But we don't. I believe that's already been made clear."

Laurel's eyes flicked over me, assessing. "Yes. Tragic. Ms. Marks's death. The missing piece. Very unfortunate."

Beau pursed his lips and looked down at the floor.

Delaney stepped in, the smooth operator. "Our clients are requesting that no additional Holloway works be displayed publicly until ownership questions are resolved."

Maybelline's face tightened. "These were donated by Joyce Holloway herself. There's no dispute—" She lifted her chin. "And the donation came with documentation. Clean and legal."

"We understand that," Delaney said. "But public exhibition could be interpreted as an assertion of control."

I blinked. "An assertion of control over two paintings you know were donated by Joyce Holloway, the heir of Neville Holloway?"

Laurel's smile sharpened, then it was as if she checked herself and her expression went grim. "Joyce's donation is precisely why we're concerned. It muddies the public narrative."

"Muddies," I repeated, hands on my hips, which were jutted out strongly to the left. "That's a polite way of saying . . . what?"

Maybelline made a small choking sound.

Delaney cut in. "We're not here to argue. We're here to formalize ownership."

"Ownership," I repeated. I was starting to sound like a parrot, but I couldn't help it.

Laurel tilted her head. "We would prefer the historical society postpones the Holloway display. Just until the matter is settled."

“Ms. Halford,” Maybelline said, wringing her hands with her clipboard locked against her chest, “the display is a highlight for the society’s fundraiser. The building is in desperate need of upgrades. The roof leaks. The wiring is—”

“Not my problem, and I mean that in the kindest way. But it’s true,” Laurel said softly, though her smile was stiff as a pair of dirty socks. “If you know anything about Bluejay Ridge lore, you’ll know my family once had these paintings. Everything is just—” she waved her hands around “—not settled. I’m sure the town will rally.”

Beau finally spoke. “We’re not trying to shut you down. Honestly. We just want to take it a little slower. Make sure every t is crossed.”

I looked at him, surprised he’d said anything at all.

He gave a small shrug. “We just don’t want mistakes.”

I’d just about had my fill of this nonsense. It was all I could do to keep my voice light. “Mistakes like what?”

“Like putting something on display that doesn’t belong to you,” Laurel said calmly, flipping her palm up. “Perhaps.”

That saying about all the air being sucked out of the room? It’s a real thing.

Maybelline stepped forward, cheeks flushed. “The paintings on display here belong to the historical society by legal donation. That is not in question.”

Brother and sister took a step back, and Delaney said, “We’ll be sending a formal notice.”

Maybelline’s mouth opened, but Laurel lifted a hand to stop her from saying whatever she was going to say.

“Maybelline,” she purred, like they were old friends, “I truly hope you will be reasonable.” Then she looked at me.

"And, Ms. Benino, if you happen to hear anything about the missing piece, do let us know."

"Perhaps the sheriff should be your resource for that kind of information."

Laurel's smile didn't waver. "Of course."

But her eyes said something else entirely, and the three of them strode away without another word.

We left the gallery room with our dignity intact—barely. I'd never been so incensed.

"What in the heavens was that?" Maybelline asked, flapping her arms as if she'd become overheated.

"Whatever it was"—and I thought of Earl's warnings—"it sounds like it's gonna turn into a knock-down, drag-out."

Maybelline looked like she might faint. "What do we do?"

I stared down the hallway toward Ralph's office. The door was open now, and it was dark inside. He'd skedaddled when no one was looking.

*What do we do?*

"We keep moving forward, my friend," I said, placing a hand on her shoulder. "And shove this little meeting to the back of our minds. They can't do anything. Joyce's donation was legit."

"I hope," Maybelline whispered.

It was curious, though, how this old feud seemed to be resurrecting itself. Back then it was over boundaries perhaps. But that was so long ago. Why would it matter now?

"Maybelline," I said quietly, "there's a storage unit. Virginia owned it, and very few people know about it. Now you, so—"

She zipped her lips shut. But they quickly reopened. "What's in the storage unit?"

"Don't ask."

She stared at me like I'd lost my mind. "I'm going to ask."

"Not here," I said, taking deep breaths in and out to steady myself. "Just . . . trust me. And let Harlan handle it."

Maybelline pressed her lips together. "Fine."

But I could tell she was already imagining worst-case scenarios. I could only hope that the storage unit would be our way through—not over, not under, but through.

As I walked out of the building, the spring-leaning air didn't revive me like it usually would have. I climbed into my Jeep and stared at the road for a long moment.

I had a feeling the storage unit wasn't just going to answer questions.

It was going to start a mighty nasty fight.

# Chapter Twenty-One

Whenever March rolled around, I started talking to my garden again. Not out loud in a dramatic way, though I've been known to scold a hydrangea or two. But more like a conversation with an old friend I hadn't seen in a while. Winter sometimes made everything look finished, exhausted, sleepy. But I knew better. The tulips and daffodils had already proven that. And the snowdrops, of course.

I was a huge fan of snowdrops, like brave little soldiers battling the remnants of cold weather. I worked around them as I always did, careful not to disturb their narrow green blades. And all the other hints of spring poking through the dirt.

But the garden beds themselves needed a refreshening.

This time last year, I'd committed to a new style—less tidy magazine spread, more abundant freedom. Curved lines instead of stiff borders. Snapdragons tucked between boxwood. Herbs dancing with the garden gnomes. The backyard was purely Betty. Theatrical, but in a charming way.

Today was about clearing space.

The old coneflower stalks snapped easily in my gloved hands. I gathered them into a pile, brushing mulch aside to expose soil that had begun, finally, to soften.

Nutty was already conducting inspections. He darted from the maple to the fence post and back again, tail flicking in judgment.

"You are not the boss of me." I shook my trowel at him.

He froze, front paws lifted like I'd insulted him in a bad way, then continued along the fence as if he couldn't care less about me or my garden plans.

I'd stopped by Serenity that morning "just to look," which in my mind is code for "prepare to spend." Tootie had been at the counter with her usual freckle-faced cuteness and sweet smile.

"Betty!" she'd shouted like she hadn't seen me just a few days ago. "You look like you're fixin' to dig."

"I always look like I'm fixin' to dig," I'd told her.

She grinned. "Then you might as well dig in color."

Which is how I'd ended up with two trays of pansies, a handful of snapdragons, some lettuce starts I really didn't want, and so many other plants that were perfect for early spring planting. I planned to jam it all in and let fly.

Now the trays and pots sat on my patio table, and every so often I'd glance over at them as I prepped the soil, feeling that small thrill that came with imagining what will bloom in a few weeks, how it will come together into its own magical forest of color.

Gardening has always been that for me—a quiet act of faith. You clear away what's spent. You loosen what's compacted. You make room. Then you plant something new and trust it to rise.

I was edging along the fence line when the thought crossed my mind—uninvited—that I'd been doing the same thing elsewhere in my life. Clearing. Loosening. Digging.

The painting. The claims to ownership. Earl's steady voice in his cabin saying how land was never just dirt.

I pushed the thought aside and leaned into the work

instead, shaving the edge of the bed clean where grass had begun its annual invasion.

I had just shifted closer to the fence—near where the snowdrops gave way to bare soil—when I heard it.

A sharp rush through the air. It registered a fraction of a second before impact. Something dark cleared the top of the fence and came at me fast.

I jerked backward on instinct. My heel caught the edge of the bed. My arms flailed in a way that would have embarrassed me if I'd had time to be embarrassed.

The object struck the ground inches from where I'd been kneeling.

I fell flat on my back. The breath left my lungs in a startled whoosh, and for a moment I lay there staring at a cloudless stretch of blue sky, trying to figure out how I'd ended up there.

*Well, that was unexpected.* My heart thudded as I rolled onto my side, pushing myself up slowly, every sense suddenly alert. I looked around.

Nutty had vanished.

The garden, which had felt warm and companionable seconds before, now felt too exposed.

And the thing that nearly took me out sat half-embedded in the soil.

A hunk of brick. Not the full brick, just a piece of one.

I glanced toward the fence. Nothing moved. No footsteps on the other side. No voice calling out a childish apology. Just stillness.

I picked up the brick. There was writing on it in black marker and neat block letters.

**BENINOS NEED TO MIND THEIR OWN BUSINESS**

For a moment, my mind refused to read it correctly.

Not Betty.

*Beninos.*

Plural.

Benino was Salvy's surname, of course. It had been mine for decades. People said it easily. Warmly. I'd never thought of it as controversial.

And yet someone had taken the time to write it. Throw it. At me.

I backed up toward the patio, where I could get a better view over the fence, and looked beyond, toward a glittering Lake Bluejay. To the left, to the right. Whoever had thrown it was gone.

My knees went a little weak anyway. My world shifted slightly off its axis. I felt lightheaded and I sat down on a wrought iron chair. Set the brick on the table and stared at it.

A message delivered with impact.

*Beninos need to mind their own business.*

The phrasing unsettled me more than anything else.

Not *you.*

Not *stop digging.*

Not even *mind your business.*

*Beninos.*

As if this wasn't new.

As if there had been other Beninos who'd needed reminding. As far as I knew, there was no Benino history in these parts.

I sat there breathing heavily, despite my attempts to remain calm. The light breeze stirred the edges of the plant tags. I had loved this yard a minute ago. Loved the work of clearing the old and making space for the new. Now I couldn't shake the feeling that someone had been watching me do it. Or at least knew I was. I glanced back at the bed I'd been edging, at the neat line I'd carved into the soil.

Have I dug too deep?

The thought came unbidden, and I almost laughed at the literalness of it.

Up until now, I had believed I was asking questions about a painting. About Virginia's death. About somebody who thought they could take what they wanted and move on. But now I believed all the lines were blurred, nothing clear anymore. This brick suggested that my name mattered to someone.

Then a slow burn of anger rose inside me. With a huff, I pushed myself up from the chair. Brushed my gloved hands together, clearing away the dirt.

If someone thought invoking the Benino name would make me step back, they had sorely miscalculated. Grandma Tater taught me better than that.

# Chapter Twenty-Two

I flung off my garden boots, shoved my socked feet into my fuzzy pink slippers, and whipped the sliding glass door open. I stepped inside and slammed the glass door closed. Nutty was sitting on the patio table, on top of the hunk of brick now, staring at me.

"Get over it," I said to him, and he turned his back on me. I'd apologize later.

*That brick . . . how dare they?*

I didn't know what bothered me more—the audacity of it or the implication. But I was as mad as a hornet.

I grabbed my phone off the pass-through counter and dialed the sheriff.

He didn't answer, and I dialed again. He answered with, "You okay?"

"No, I am certainly not okay. Where are you right now?"

"I'm at the storage unit," he said.

Before he had the chance to get clever with me, I said, "I'm coming there now."

"No," he said immediately.

I narrowed my eyes at my kitchen wall as if it were him. "Excuse me?"

"You heard me."

"Harlan," I said, trying for calm but my clipped words probably wiped that right out, "someone just threw a brick at my head."

Silence.

Then, "You all right?"

"I'm fine," I snapped. "But I'm not fine. They wrote my name on it. Plural, as in Beninos. It was a warning."

Another beat.

"I warned you about the danger—"

"I was gardening in my backyard!" I screeched. "There shouldn't have been a safer place for me!" I didn't like the way I sounded, but I was close to crying. I sucked in a shuddering breath, adding, "Sorry for yelling."

A long exhale on the other end. "Stay inside the house. I can't have you rolling up here and potentially contaminating a scene."

"I won't touch anything. I'll keep my hands in my pockets like a kindergarten field trip. But I'm coming."

"I know you're upset—"

"Oh, boy howdy, I'm more than upset. I want answers!" I planted my free hand on my hip. "No one gets to invoke my husband's name—my name—and you to tell me to sit at home drinking some dagnabbit herbal tea."

"Dagnabbit, huh? Maybe something stronger would be in order?"

"I'll bring a bottle and we can share, but I am not sitting here. Harlan, please."

He spoke to someone nearby—couldn't hear what he'd said—then came back to me. "Fine, but you listen to me. You come out here and you do exactly what I say. Exactly."

"Deal."

"I mean it."

"I heard you the first time."

"You drive straight here," he said. "No detours. You don't

stop at Serenity, you don't stop to chat with Jolene, and you don't bring Trudy."

"She would love that though."

"I know she would. That's why you're not doing it. And when you get here, you stay in your Jeep until I tell you otherwise."

This all was suspiciously reasonable. Perhaps the man had a heart after all. "I can handle that."

"And you bring that brick."

I blinked. "You want the brick?"

"Yes," he said. "It's evidence, Betty."

"Well," I muttered, "I'm glad my near-concussion can be useful."

"Wrap it in something. Don't smear it."

"I get it! See you soon."

This time I hung up on him first.

I stared at my phone for half a second, then marched to the pantry, grabbed a brown paper bag, and stepped outside. I approached the hunk of brick warily, picked it up with my thumb and forefinger, and quickly slid it inside the bag. Then I grabbed my keys and headed for the Jeep.

A prickling feeling settled over me halfway down the sidewalk.

I turned, went back up the steps, and locked the door, including the deadbolt.

# Chapter Twenty-Three

Virginia's storage unit was just past town where the highway widened and the scenery got less charming and more functional. Feed store. A gas station that sold boiled peanuts in a big old pot near the front door. A used car lot with flags snapping in the wind. Then a narrow gravel drive with a hand-painted sign that read:

**BLUEJAY STORAGE**
**LOCALS OWN IT**
**SECURITY CAMERAS ON SIGHT**

*Well, close enough,* and I smirked at the wording. The "security cameras" part had a little starburst drawn underneath it for emphasis.

I slowed as I turned in.

Rows of outdoor roll-up units stretched out like metal teeth. A white office trailer sat near the front gate, with a small porch and a wind chime made of beer cans. A man in a ball cap stood outside talking to Harlan, who was planted in front of him with that exact posture he used when he wanted a person to understand that their day was about to get inconvenient.

Harlan saw my Jeep and lifted one hand. Not a wave. A stop sign.

I parked along the edge and stayed put like he'd ordered. Hands on the wheel. Paper bag on the passenger seat, the brick calling my name—literally. My heart rate was still not cooperating with my directive to chill the dickens out.

Harlan walked over and opened my door. His eyes flicked to the bag. "That it?"

I handed it to him.

He took it carefully, pulled out the brick hunk, and read it. He lifted his gaze and studied me. "Where were you hit?"

"I was not hit. I was nearly hit. Thanks to my fast reflexes and well-honed gut instincts, I was able to roll out of the way when I heard it come swooshing down at me."

His mouth twitched a bit.

"Don't you laugh," I warned, wagging my finger at him.

Then we both started chuckling.

"But this isn't funny," he said, putting on his stern face again.

"No it isn't," I agreed, also sobering.

He handed me the brick. "I'll collect it before we leave."

"Can we have a look inside that unit now?"

He nodded, stepping aside. "You can get out. But you stay right next to me."

"Am I on a leash?"

"Basically."

I climbed out and shut the door.

Harlan nodded toward the man in the ball cap. "This is Mr. Larkin. He runs the place."

"Howdy," Mr. Larkin said. His demeanor clearly said he didn't want to be involved in anyone's drama, but here we all were. He looked uncomfortable, scratching his chin, shifting his feet, not knowing what to do with his hands.

"Hi," I said, just a normal woman who didn't just have her surname weaponized by flying masonry.

Harlan said to the man, "Unit twenty-seven is Ms. Marks's, correct?"

"Yes sir," he said. "Paid up through April. Never late."

"Any family come by?" Harlan asked.

"Did she have any?" I whispered, and he shushed me.

Mr. Larkin scratched his cheek. "Not that I've seen. And I don't give out information to anybody without paperwork. That's how I keep peace around here."

"Cameras?" Harlan asked.

Mr. Larkin shrugged in a way that did not inspire confidence. "Got a few."

Harlan gave him a look.

"They work," Mr. Larkin clarified quickly. "Most of the time." He gestured down the row. "It's over there."

We walked in silence between the units, our footsteps crunching on gravel. In the distance, a chain-link gate rattled in the wind. In the other distance, a dog barked like it was about to chew someone's leg off.

Unit twenty-seven was halfway down, and it looked exactly like every other one: dented metal, faded numbers, small padlock—hardly a deterrent to anyone who wanted to enter. I could snap that with my garden shears.

Harlan walked closer, pulling on some latex gloves, and studied the lock.

"Has it been tampered with?" I asked, not able to see it because of his big shoulders.

Mr. Larkin approached us from behind like a ghost. I hadn't even heard his footsteps on the gravel. "Er, forgot to mention . . . I've got the gate key and camera access, but each unit lock is private, as you can see."

Harlan nodded at him. “Appreciate your help. You should go on back to the office now.”

Mr. Larkin looked undecided for a moment, then turned and strode away.

We watched until he was out of sight. Then Harlan leaned back down toward the lock and said, “See this? Scratches.”

I squinted. “Could be from keys.”

“Could,” he said. “Could also be from someone trying to pick it or snap it.”

My stomach did a little twirl. This unit was going to solve everything—unless someone else had gotten to it first. “You think they got in?”

“Maybe,” he said. “Or they tried and couldn’t.”

“And if they couldn’t—” I started.

Harlan shot me a warning look, then glanced over my shoulder.

I zipped it and turned.

Mr. Larkin was back with a pair of bolt cutters. “Sheriff, I can cut it if you need me to.”

I looked at Harlan. “Do it.”

Harlan looked at the lock again. “Not yet.”

He pulled out a small evidence flashlight and angled it along the seam where the door met the frame.

Then he stood and looked at the ground.

“Here,” he said.

I followed his gaze.

In the grit near the door was a faint impression—a tread mark, partial and shallow, like someone had stepped there when the gravel was damp.

Harlan crouched. “Boot print.”

My pulse ticked up. “Size?”

He studied it, then shot me a knowing look. "Ohhh, I'd say about a ten."

I gasped. There'd been a similar boot print outside of Virginia's window. *But what's the big deal? A size ten doesn't point to anyone specifically—it could point to almost anyone. Man or woman. Not a giant. Not a tiny.*

*But still . . .*

"Do you think it's the same person?" I asked.

Harlan didn't answer right away. He photographed it, then set a small marker beside it.

"Mr. Larkin," he said, "do you keep a list of who's got gate access and when the cameras went down?"

"Yes sir," Mr. Larkin said. "I can pull it."

"Do that," Harlan said. "And pull camera footage. From the last week."

Mr. Larkin nodded quickly, seeming happy to have been assigned a task.

When he walked off, Harlan stood and looked at me.

"You see why I didn't want you here?" he asked.

"Yes," I said. "Because now I want to do something dumb."

"Exactly."

I crossed my arms. "So what now?"

Harlan reached into his pocket and pulled out a set of keys. "I got the key from her personal effects," he said. "It wasn't labeled. But . . ."

He slid it in, turned it carefully, and the padlock clicked open. "It fits."

I could have knocked him over with the biggest bear hug he'd ever had. I was elated. "You're the best!" I squeaked.

"Can't argue with you there," he muttered, and I swear he almost smiled.

Then he pulled the lock free and set it in an evidence bag.

As he slowly lifted the roll-up door, the metal rattled, and the smell hit me first—dust, must, cardboard, old fabric, and that faint hint of mouse that old barns, basements, attics, and storage units seemed to have.

Inside, Virginia's life sat in stacks.

A folded card table. A couple plastic bins labeled CHRISTMAS and LINENS in tidy black letters. A wide-eyed mannequin, of all things. Boxes. Banker's boxes. A framed mirror. A lamp.

No painting. And nothing screamed, "Here is information about a valuable painting."

Harlan stepped in first. I hovered at the threshold like a child at the edge of a swimming pool, anxious to dive in.

"Don't touch," he said without looking at me.

"I won't," I promised. Mostly because my hands were trembling a little, and I didn't want to drop anything.

Harlan moved toward a banker's box near the back. It was taped shut, and written on the top in Virginia's neat hand were two words:

WINTER GARDEN

"You see that?" Harlan pointed at the box.

"I see it," I whispered.

He photographed the label, then carefully cut the tape.

Inside were folders. File sleeves. A few manila envelopes. A zippered pouch the color of oatmeal. And a small padded mailer—empty—like something had been slid out and the envelope tucked back into place.

Harlan didn't rush. He photographed it, then lifted the padded mailer between two gloved fingers.

"What's that?" I asked.

"Could be nothing," he said. "Could be something someone didn't want found."

He set it down and opened the folder underneath.

Photocopies. Notes. A typed letterhead from a bank. A receipt stub.

He didn't show me the paperwork right away. He just stared down at it. "Well, I'll be . . ."

I tried to get a look, but he turned away from me. "Be what? What is it?"

Finally, he held up the receipt stub. "Safe deposit box."

My heart hammered. "Virginia had a safe deposit box?"

"Looks like it," he said. Then he reached into the folder and pulled out a small envelope.

On the front, in Virginia's handwriting: *If Anything Happens.*

Harlan opened it carefully.

Inside was a key. A small brass key. Not a storage key.

A bank key.

"Oh," I whispered.

He cocked an eyebrow. "This is what someone came for."

"And they didn't get it," I said, hope flickering.

Harlan's gaze slid to the rest of the unit—a mess but there was something ...

And then I saw the *something*. Boxes slightly shifted, dust disturbed in a narrow track near the back, like someone had moved through there carefully trying not to make a mess.

"Maybe they did get it," he said quietly.

"No way. Why would they risk putting it back?" I shook my head. "They'd have pocketed it and run."

Harlan snapped his fingers and pointed at me, nodding, like that was the first sensible thing I'd said all day. He reached into the zippered pouch and opened it.

Inside were three things: a few printed photos on glossy paper—close-ups of brushstrokes and a corner of canvas, not the full image—a simple hand-drawn sketch of three rectangles labeled *Left/Middle/Right*, and a sticky note in Virginia's tidy hand: *Don't display until this is settled.*

I swallowed. "Maybe she sensed a fight was coming."

"Seems so. More like she knew someone was going to come looking." He scanned the unit again.

"Maybe this is why she hesitated to donate the painting," I said, voice tight. "She knew it would stir people up."

Harlan stared at the key in his gloved hand. "Now somebody's throwing bricks about the Beninos."

"And that."

He grunted, clearly still thinking.

"Can we go to the bank?" I asked.

He tucked the key back into the envelope and slid it into an evidence bag. "We can. And we will."

"Great. Let's get out of here—"

"But not with you leading the parade," he added.

I opened my mouth.

He held up a finger. "You did good. You told me. You brought evidence. You didn't touch anything in here."

"I deserve a big gold medal," I muttered. "Or at least insider information."

"You deserve to go home," he said. "I'm sending out a cruiser to watch the house. Whoever threw that brick wanted you rattled. And I'm not giving them the satisfaction of you being out in the open any longer than necessary."

I stared at him. “This is my life.”

“I know,” he said, and for a second his voice softened. “That’s why I’m taking it seriously.”

From down the row, Mr. Larkin jogged back toward us, holding a phone.

“Sheriff Brooks,” he called. “Cameras got somethin’. Not great but . . . somethin’.”

Harlan’s posture tightened instantly. “In your Jeep,” he said. He shot me a glance that did not invite a retort of any kind.

I wanted to argue. I did. But I also wanted to live. So I backed out of the unit and walked quickly to my Jeep.

Through the windshield, I watched Harlan stand with Mr. Larkin, looking down at the phone screen.

Even from here, I could see it in Harlan’s face.

Whatever was on that footage mattered.

# Chapter Twenty-Four

Hank Whitfield had a standing rule about our O'Malley's cocktail nights: no gossip until the first drink landed on the table.

I broke it before my butt even hit the barstool.

"I'm not ordering anything with brick dust on my hands," I told him, sliding in next to him at the bar. I'd already filled him in on the brick before we got here.

Hank blinked once, slow. "Ma'am. I asked you—very kindly—to save the drama until after the olives."

"I can't," I said. "The drama is currently in my purse. Fighting against the seams of the paper bag. Can't you hear it?"

Rhonda appeared like she'd been summoned by the word *drama*. "What are we drinking?"

"Whiskey, top shelf," I said automatically. "Neat."

Hank's eyebrows shot up. "Now that's what I'm talking about. I'll have the same."

Rhonda's gaze sharpened. "Betty, you okay?"

I didn't hide my feelings easily. I didn't even try, to be honest. At least not often. But I said, "I'm fine," which was becoming my least believable line.

Rhonda didn't ask twice. She slid us our drinks, then leaned in with that bartender stare that could make a grown man confess to shoplifting beef jerky in ninth grade.

Or woman. Not that I knew anyone like that.

"Tell me," she demanded, and I told her about the brick, but not without a long sigh first.

"You got a bruise?" she asked.

"No."

"You got a concussion?"

"No. But I do have a cruiser parked outside my house now."

"You got a reason you're sitting here instead of home where you're safe?"

I opened my mouth, but Hank beat me to it.

"She needed a breather. Besides, I can protect her." He lifted his glass.

I lifted mine. "I don't need protecting. But thanks anyway."

We clinked.

For a moment—just a moment—the room felt like itself again. Warm, and loud, and family. A cozy hum that almost, *almost* made me forget Virginia had been murdered and a brick had been aimed at my skull.

Then the front door opened, and Trudy Carter swept in like a storm.

She spotted us and marched straight over, cane leading the way.

"Lord help me," Hank murmured. "Here comes Trouble with a capital T."

Trudy ignored him and pointed at me. "You."

"What?" I asked.

"You okay?"

"I'm fine," I said again, because I had no other script.

Trudy's eyes narrowed. "You don't look fine."

"That's because somebody tried to knock me out with construction materials," I said, and Hank choked on his drink.

Rhonda snapped her towel at my shoulder. "Betty."

"What? It's the truth."

Trudy slid into the booth beside me like she owned it. "I know about the brick."

Hank's gaze bounced between us. "Do y'all have a newsletter I'm not subscribed to?"

Trudy leaned closer. "I also went to that storage place."

I froze. "You did what?"

She flicked a hand at Rhonda. "I'll have what they're having." Then she turned back to me. "Somebody had to put a little hot sauce on this whole mess."

"Trudy . . ." Not sure exactly what that meant.

"Don't you Trudy me," she said. "You went and got yourself bricked. I'm not leaving this to Sheriff Brooks. The only reason he knows about half of it is because of me. Virginia was my friend, as are you, Betty. Now hush and listen."

I honestly loved it when Trudy got her gander up. "What did you find out?"

"Larkin's cameras caught a vehicle," she said. "Not great footage. Grainy. Angle's wrong. But clear enough for one thing."

Hank leaned forward. "Which is?"

She ignored him and looked me dead in the eye. "It's a newer SUV, looks like one of them Enchiladas."

"Escalades?" Rhonda guessed.

She tapped the side of her nose. "That's the one."

"Is that bad?"

"Well it is when they come into the grounds late, real late, then sit there right in front of Unit 27."

"The cameras showed that?" I felt the room tilt a fraction.

"Sure do. And then . . ." She leaned in and eyeballed me, Hank, and Rhonda in turn. "And then someone gets out."

Hank slapped the countertop. “Now, that’s something. Can you see their face?”

Trudy scoffed. “Please. If I could see their face, I’d already have them hogtied in my trunk.”

*That’s no lie.*

“You can’t see much. But you can see the shape,” Trudy said, taking a fast swig of her drink that Rhonda had just set on the bar. “Medium height. Hood up. Moving quick-like.”

My mind flashed to Virginia’s study. The bent screen. The open window. The mess.

*Same person? It has to be.*

“And the unit?” I asked. “Did they get in?”

“That’s the part Larkin couldn’t say for sure,” Trudy said. “The camera catches the SUV rolling in and that hoodie walking straight down Virginia’s row—but Unit 27 sits in a little blind spot. You see the figure disappear behind the units, then a few minutes later, they come back out the same way and leave.”

I stared into my glass. “Why would Larkin tell you any of this?”

Trudy’s mouth twitched. “Because he has a mother.”

Hank snorted. “What does that mean?”

“It means,” Trudy said sweetly, “that when I asked him politely, he tried to act like he shouldn’t tell me because it was in the hands of the sheriff. When I asked him like a woman who helped raise him, he remembered just fine.”

I could see it in my mind’s eye now. Poor Larkin. Trudy’s superpower was her commanding presence.

Rhonda set down a bowl of olives. “So what’s the sheriff doing with it?”

Trudy waved a hand. “Whatever sheriffs do, more than likely.”

“Did you tell him?”

“No, and no one here is either.” She narrowed her eyes at us.

We all nodded like bobbleheads.

“But I will tell him myself, and that I told you. I’m not having secrets inside secrets. Not when people are killing my friends or tossing bricks at their heads.”

I exhaled, trying to steady my thoughts. “So we have an SUV, a hooded person, and a storage unit key that leads to a bank box.”

Trudy froze. “What have you not told me?”

So I filled them in on what Harlan and I had seen . . . and discovered. That Virginia had a safe deposit box, and now we had the key.

“Someone’s going down, and soon, Trudy seethed. “And let’s not forget the warning that referred to the *Beninos*—plural—keeping to their own business.”

Hank’s face shifted. Just slightly. It was quick, but I caught it.

I nudged him. “What?”

Hank blinked. “What?”

I leaned forward. “You just did a thing.”

He frowned. “I did not.”

“Ha!” Trudy tossed back her drink then slammed the glass on the counter. “Oh, you did a thing. I saw it too.”

Hank held up both hands. “Maybe I did a small thing. But here’s why. I’ve heard that name before.”

My heart beat harder. “Benino?”

"Not referring to you," he said quickly. "But the last name."

Trudy's eyes sharpened. "And you're just now realizing it?"

"Hey, I've just been invited to the party. Give me a break." He shook out his shoulders like he was a prize fighter. "My daddy used to do contract work. Up toward the ridge, back in the day. He'd come home and talk about old surveys and old families like it was the weather."

My mouth went dry. "And?"

"And I remember him mentioning—once—some fella from long ago. A name on a paper. Not Halford or Holloway. Not even Brooks." Hank looked at me. "I would swear on my life it was *Benino*."

It seemed like all the buzz in the bar faded to nothing. I was in a tomb of silence.

We all stopped moving.

Trudy leaned in so close I could smell peppermint. "You remember anything else?"

Hank shook his head slowly. "No. Not yet. But my daddy kept stuff. Old notebooks. Old receipts. Invoices, you name it. He'd write everything down."

My pulse jumped. "Do you still have all of it?"

"Maybe," he said. "They're in boxes at my place. In the garage. I haven't looked at them in years."

Trudy pointed at him like he was a suspect and a savior at the same time. "You're going to look tonight."

Hank blinked. "Tonight?"

"Yes," Trudy said. "Tonight."

Hank glanced at me. "Is she always this bossy when she drinks?"

Trudy paid the tab for everyone. "Son, I haven't even gotten started."

Hank cleared his throat. "Okay. Fine. I'll look. But y'all are *not* coming into my garage acting like it's an episode of *Dateline*."

Trudy smiled sweetly. "Sure we are."

# Chapter Twenty-Five

Twenty minutes later, we were standing in Hank's garage under harsh overhead light, staring at a stack of dusty, warped boxes.

Hank rubbed his hands together and nodded toward the pile. "These were my daddy's. Been sitting in this back corner . . . well, forever it seems. I haven't touched 'em since he, uh, died."

Trudy's expression softened for exactly half a second. Then she snapped right back into business. "Let's do it."

"I don't know what y'all think you're gonna find," Hank muttered, tugging open the top box. "My daddy did contractor work. Drywall. Roof patches. Outbuildings. He wasn't Indiana Jones."

"Men who write things down are always Indiana Jones," Trudy said.

I stifled a laugh and stepped closer.

The box was full of old folders and spiral notebooks and all kinds of little pieces of paper, including folded napkins with measurements written on them.

Hank pulled out a notebook and flipped it open.

His shoulders loosened a fraction, like he'd found a familiar rhythm in the mess. "Okay. . . okay. Here we go."

"You got a notebook for each job?" I asked.

Hank nodded. "Daddy wrote everything down. Every nail. Every board. Every name. He didn't trust his memory."

"I respect that," I said. "My memory is a liar." *Not true.*

Hank flipped through pages, his finger trailing down lines of cramped handwriting.

"Halford," he said suddenly.

My spine tightened. "What?"

He held the page up. "Here . . . *Halford barn – replace hinge. Paid cash.*"

Trudy gave a short grunt. "Keep going."

Hank did, turning another page, then another, then one more. He frowned, stopping on a page. He tapped a line twice.

"Here," he said.

I leaned in.

Trudy almost edge me out, but I held firm.

Hank read out loud, slow:

*"Benino Place – ridge side. Patch roof seam. Outbuilding repair. Don't park by the creek."*

For a second my brain refused to cooperate.

Benino Place?

Like something that existed before I ever moved here.

My mouth went dry. "My Beninos?"

Trudy's eyes sharpened. "Would have to be. Or else, why throw a brick at you warning about the Beninos?"

Hank flipped back a page and pointed at a date scribbled in the margin. "Date's 1973-ish."

I stared at the words until they started to blur.

Benino Place.

Trudy crossed her arms. "And where was it?"

Hank flipped a few pages farther, then stopped again.

"Here," he said, and read, "Turnoff – Benino Road."

My heart gave a couple of hard thumps. For a second I

felt untethered, like I'd stepped into a story that started long before I arrived.

"There's a Benino Road?" I asked.

Hank shrugged. "There was. Seemed like common knowledge, the way he wrote it. But that doesn't mean it's still called that. Roads get renamed. People move. Things change."

Trudy's gaze locked on mine. "Well, that's something, isn't it?"

It sure was.

She lifted her chin. "Y'all must have ticked someone off. Or at least someone remembers it enough to throw a brick and write a warning about the *Beninos* minding their own business. What a kicker!"

My stomach did a slow roll. Feeling faint, I steadied myself on a box.

"Okay," I said through shallow breaths. "Here's what I'm going to do."

Trudy pointed at me. "You're going to call Harlan."

"Yes," I said. "I'm going to call Harlan."

"I'll leave everything here," Hank said, placing the notebook inside the box, "as is, in case Harlan wants to check things out."

I pulled out my phone. "Good," I said. "Because whether this is nothing or everything . . . it's got my name on it."

I hit the call button.

My knees gave out and my vision got staticky and Trudy swiped the phone from my hand.

While I drank a glass of water, courtesy of Hank, I could hear Trudy giving Harlan the 4-1-1.

# Chapter Twenty-Six

By the time I got home, I was still feeling shaky. Hank and Trudy had put me in a wheelchair she kept in her car "for emergencies," and rolled me all the way to my porch steps.

The cruiser was still parked out front. The deputy—a new one, thirtysomething and handsome as can be—sat behind the wheel with a coffee in one hand and his phone in the other. He'd lifted two fingers at me when I wheeled past.

I assured Trudy and Hank I was fine and sent them on their way. They'd pleaded with me to allow them to carry me inside and tuck me under a blanket on the couch with a soothing tea, but enough was enough.

When the coast was clear, I shuffled to the cruiser. "Any excitement, Deputy Vega?"

"No, ma'am," he said. "All is well."

"Let's keep it that way." I hesitated, then added, "Sheriff wanted the brick. I still have it. Will you give it to him for me?"

"Yes, ma'am. You need help?"

I waved him off. Leaning into the passenger's side of the Jeep, I grabbed the bag with the heels of my hands. I hurried back to the deputy and dropped it onto the seat like it was a rabid squirrel.

Vega gave me a thumbs-up. "We'll get it into evidence."

"Good," I said, though I didn't feel good about a single thing.

I locked up my Jeep, then went inside and checked every

lock on every door and window. My heart was still in a sprint as I stood in my quiet living room and tried to “feel” if someone had intruded. Not that I doubted the deputy’s skills, but . . . well, I trusted no one.

My phone rang as I held it, and I saw it was Harlan. I answered on the first ring. “Tell me you found something.”

“I found something,” he said in a monotone voice.

That man could make “good news” sound like an obituary.

“I need you down here at the station,” Harlan said. “You got time?”

I let out a slow breath. “Tonight?”

“Yes, tonight.”

I glanced toward my bedroom door, aching to lie down and forget the day. “Give me a reason I won’t hate.”

A pause. “Virginia left something in her safety deposit box,” he said.

“Harlan, that’s not exactly news.”

“Your name’s in it.”

I flopped back onto the couch, my feet bouncing up in the air when I hit the cushions hard. “That’s not what I thought you would say. Not even in the ballpark. Give me ten.”

---

The sheriff was waiting for me by the station’s main entrance to let me in. My legs felt a little steadier, though my nerves had been thoroughly dipped in oil and Southern fried.

“Harlan.”

“Betty.”

That was the extent of the pleasantries as we walked back to his office.

Harlan sat in his big chair, sleeves rolled up, a file spread open across his desk. "Sit," he said, gesturing at the chair across from him.

I sat.

He got right to the point. He pushed a white envelope in my direction, the flap facing up, and it had been opened. I reached for it. But he didn't let it go. "In a moment."

"Okay." I withdrew my hand. "You're being awfully dramatic. Where's the part about the Beninos?"

"Crimes don't get solved by rushing the evidence. Plus, I like a good drama as much as anyone." He smiled, a real smile, and that settled me somehow. He wasn't made of stone, after all.

"That envelope is addressed to me," he said. "To be opened if anything happened to Virginia."

"What did it say?"

He ignored my question, instead holding up an 8x10 manila envelope that had also been in the file folder. "This is what she was working on." With a flourish, he pulled out a copy of a painting and held it up for me to see.

I recognized it immediately as one by Neville Holloway. The brushstrokes and style were undeniably his. But which painting?

I gasped. "Is it . . .?" I reached for it, but he set it down on the desk and held it firmly with his finger.

"It is. A picture of the second painting in the Winter Garden series."

But it wasn't just a photo of the painting. It had pencil markings—notes along the edges and lines drawn this way and that.

"She was studying it like a map," I said.

"That's exactly what she was doing."

He reached for another page. This was a photocopy of what looked like an old property map. Faded lines, handwritten labels, numbers, coordinates . . . things that might've made sense to a surveyor and absolutely no one else.

I studied it, nonetheless. I loved old records. That was what had drawn me to volunteering for the historical society in the first place. Possibly the worst idea I'd ever had, in retrospect.

Then he set a third sheet next to it on the desk. A cleaner, modern version of the map.

"Current records," he said, tapping the newer page. "What the land looks like now. Or at least what it says it looks like."

"I'm not much of a map reader, but . . ." I brought my readers down to my nose and scooted to the edge of my seat, "they don't match."

"Not quite." He pointed to a section near the edge of both maps. "See this here?"

On the older map was a thin, uneven line cutting along the back edge of what must've once been part of the Holloway property.

On the newer one, that line was gone. Almost.

There was a tiny area marked off on the modern map, presumably by Virginia. She had circled it in pencil. Several times. A name was included in that circle.

"Benino," I whispered.

Harlan nodded. "The Benino family's little slice of land," he said. "Doesn't amount to much. Never did. But it sits right along where that old boundary used to be."

I stared at it, then at the copy of the painting again. There, low in the composition, was the old stone wall, so slight one might not notice it. I gasped. "Holloway was sending a message about the property lines."

"I think so."

I leaned closer, my pulse picking up. The line in the painting matched the line on the old map in the same stubborn, crooked way. Not *exact* exact, but near enough to make my skin prickle. Virginia had not been imagining things. She had been reading the land through the painting—and once I saw it, I couldn't unsee it either.

"Salvy's name being there, my married name . . . That's quite a coincidence."

"That it is."

"Bizarre, really." My mind whirred, trying to understand. "I feel certain Salvy would have mentioned it if he'd known about family land in Georgia. They're more of a New York crew—with a massive ancestry. Lots of branches on that tree. Still, I don't think he had any idea about this."

"More than likely." Harlan leaned back slightly, studying me. "Virginia discovered it, maybe even fairly recently, and she'd been debating what to do with that painting."

"Clearly, she'd wanted to donate it, but then second-guessed herself at the last minute," I added.

He picked up the thread. "Thinking about what kind of a stir it might cause, because as we have learned, the Halfords and Holloways didn't always get along. They had frequent disputes over boundaries and whatever else. So, Virginia hid the painting and left us these clues should anything ever happen to her before she made her final decision."

"She certainly didn't make it easy. Presuming it wasn't stolen, does she say where she hid the painting?" I asked, hopeful.

"No, she does not. It seems like it's something we were meant to figure out."

He picked up the white envelope and handed it to me. "Go ahead."

I took it with a trembling hand. Turned it over. It had been addressed to Harlan Brooks. I withdrew the folded piece of paper, opened it. Upon seeing Virginia's careful handwriting, I got choked up and covered my mouth briefly. She was speaking to us from beyond the grave.

*If anything should happen to me, Sheriff Harlan Brooks is to review the enclosed materials in full, as I have no next of kin. The decision as to how to proceed is his and his alone.*

*The second painting of Neville Holloway's Winter Garden series, which has been hidden by me, as directed by its prior owner, Ruby Pearl McCallister, does not reflect current land records, but an earlier configuration that has been altered over time.*

*The Benino parcel appears repeatedly at the edge of these discrepancies. It may be insignificant in value, but not in placement.*

*Still, that may be enough.*

*Roberta Tater Benino should be made aware. I do not believe she is involved in any wrongdoing, but her name has now entered the same chain of records.*

*As Harlan Brooks's family is part of this town's legacy, I trust he will do the right thing with both legacy and safety in mind.*

*— Virginia Marks, of sound mind and body*

It was dated just weeks before her death.

I lowered the page. "She wrote, 'That may be enough.' But enough for what?"

Harlan didn't soften it. "Enough for someone to think you're a problem."

A chill worked its way down my spine. "She thought I was in danger." Virginia had known enough to be frightened, and maybe enough to know she was running out of time. "And she was in danger. But who would kill over—"

"Land?" He raised both eyebrows. "You're kidding me, right?"

I let out a shaky breath. "I still can't believe it. All this because my family owns a sliver of land nobody's cared about in fifty years?"

"Clearly, Betty—" he placed his palms firmly on the desk "—someone cares very much."

I looked back down at the map. That tiny, meaningless strip of land didn't feel so meaningless anymore.

And underneath the fear, there was something else. Not pride exactly. Not yet. But a strange pull in my chest at seeing Salvy's people—his name, my name—still sitting there in the middle of a story that had been . . . untold, in a way.

Harlan's jaw shifted slightly. "That's the other thing I'd learned recently, but now it makes so much more sense. There are some plans in the works for that area," he said. "Plans big enough that the last thing the developers need is questions about where one property ends and another begins."

"What is it?" I said, breathless.

"Some sort of spa. The Halfords are one of the investors, as it involves a **big chunk** of their land, which includes the Benino land. Plenty of other people are involved too, so I'm not pointing fingers. If somebody starts digging into old boundaries, it can slow things down. Complicate things. Cost more money. Might even halt the development entirely."

"And Virginia was digging."

"She was, yes."

I swallowed. "And now I'm . . . what? Standing on the edge of it? What do we do?"

He pulled all the information together and tucked it back into the file folder. "You will do nothing but stay safe until this is all sorted."

*Easier said than done..*

# Chapter Twenty-Seven

A special meeting had been called. Despite my protests, Harlan had insisted on escorting me himself.

When we stepped into the Bluejay Ridge Historical Society, I knew two things for certain.

One, this was going to be a free-for-all.

And two, nobody in that room trusted anybody else.

Or maybe that was just me—running on too little sleep and too much information.

Everyone seemed to be on edge, their demeanors dark, like a storm had rolled in and hovered right inside this room.

Maybelline Griggs stood near the center table, lips pressed thin, her clipboard clutched tightly to her chest. She did that a lot lately, as if she had information she didn't want anyone to see. And maybe she did.

Ralph Jenkins sat off to the side, still looking pale but he was upright and shaven at least. Though he'd tried mightily to stay two steps removed from the very work he'd been hired to do, there were no more excuses to be had.

Across the room stood Attorney Delaney, appearing more unlikable than I could have imagined. For the first time, I realized he looked a bit like a well-dressed weasel. Alert and ready to bite if cornered.

Near him stood the Halford siblings. Polished, composed and carrying the quiet confidence of people who'd never once had to wonder how things would turn out for them.

Joyce Holloway lingered near the back wall, one hand resting lightly on the edge of a table, her expression unreadable. I wondered if she regretted donating the duo. Or did she have a vindictive side that was not immediately evident? Had she made the donation with ill intent—to rip open old wounds?

And then there was Dr. Mercer, leaning against a wall, tapping her pen against a legal pad. Her eyes scanned the room repeatedly. Taking notes, I realized—not on paper, but in her mind.

I, on the other hand, felt underdressed, underprepared, and entirely too involved.

Maybelline cleared her throat. "Now that everyone is here—"

"We're still waiting on clarity," Delaney cut in smoothly. "Which, I was under the impression, was the purpose of this gathering."

His voice was polite, but he was a lawyer. Polite was how they started, then . . . cue knife across the throat.

Or in the back.

Oh, Virginia, what have you done?

"This is a historical society," Ralph said, his voice thin. Whether effects from his flu or from his wanting to be anywhere but here, I wasn't sure. "Clarity takes time."

"And yet," Lauren Halford said, "time is exactly what we don't have."

"And why is that?" I stepped forward, but Harlan pulled me back.

Lauren did not respond, but there was an exchange of gazes that dominoed around the room.

No one wanted to be the first to say it out loud. But everyone knew something had changed.

"Perhaps," Dr. Mercer said, "we should define the concern."

"Oh, I think the concern is quite clear," Delaney replied. "There appears to be a growing suggestion that existing land records are . . . inaccurate. Thanks to Ms. Virginia Marks's poking into things that maybe weren't her concern. And look where that got her."

A rumble of murmurs. The outsider had crossed a line.

"Not necessarily inaccurate," Maybelline quickly corrected. "Just . . . er . . . under review."

"That's a generous way of putting it," Harlan said in low voice, leaning down quite a bit so I could hear him.

"I want to talk about that spa," I whispered back. "Let's get it out in the open and cut to the chase."

"In due time, Betty. Let it unfold."

Joyce Holloway spoke then, her voice soft but steady. "Virginia wasn't someone who did things on a whim," she said. "If she had concerns about donating that painting, or about boundaries or whatever, it was for a reason. And I think it's awful that you, Mr. Delaney, or anyone would suggest a murder victim had basically deserved what she got."

Another ripple of hushed voices moved through the room.

Delaney didn't look at her. "Not what I said. Is anyone taking the minutes?" He looked around to find blank faces. He shrugged. "I'm sure Ms. Marks had her interests," he continued. "But we must be careful not to confuse curiosity with fact."

That did it.

"Curiosity doesn't usually get someone killed," I said.

Harlan didn't even move to stop me. Progress.

Beau Halford began to pace, hands behind his back, as if he were the lawyer. "With respect," he said, "we're here because there's been talk about boundaries. Old maps. Interpretations of a painting. The missing painting, and the three paintings in the Winter Garden series as a whole."

"And ..?" Maybelline said, looking more worried by the second.

"And," he continued, "we have a development project already in motion. Investors. Timelines. Commitments."

There it was.

No one said spa. But everyone heard it.

"So it's about money," someone shouted from the corner.

Maybelline held up a hand. "Mr. Halford, this society has a responsibility to preserve accurate history."

"And we have a responsibility," Lauren jumped in, "to ensure that outdated or misinterpreted information doesn't create unnecessary complications."

"Unnecessary?" Ralph repeated, a flicker of irritation cutting through his exhaustion. Finally. "You're talking about land ownership."

"Mere speculation that there is anything amiss," Lauren countered.

Harlan stepped forward just enough to shift the balance of the room.

"It's not speculation," he said. "We've got a discrepancy between historical documentation and current records. On paper. Not mere curiosity."

"And what exactly does that discrepancy amount to?" Delaney asked.

Harlan didn't answer right away.

Instead, he glanced at me.

Just once.

That was all the invitation I needed.

I stepped forward. Every eye in the room landed on me.

"Well," I said, keeping my voice as steady as I could manage, "it amounts to a very small, very unimpressive piece of land that apparently nobody cared about—until now."

"Ms. Benino, you're still a newcomer—" Beau started.

But Harlan held up his hand and said, "Let her finish."

"I'm talking about the Benino parcel," I said.

Gasps all around. My words had dropped into the room like a stone into still water.

"How is that possible?" Maybelline asked, her eyes jumping back and forth between me and Harlan. Then she just froze, mouth hanging open.

Except one person.

There was a flicker of recognition. Gone almost as quickly as it appeared. But I'd caught it.

It was exactly what I'd been looking for.

I glanced at Harlan, who'd seen it too. I knew he did. Because his attention shifted, not broadly or obviously, but just enough.

Zeroing in.

"Like I said," I added lightly, though my pulse had picked up, "not exactly prime real estate."

"No," Delaney said smoothly. "It isn't."

"And yet," I said, tilting my head just slightly, "it could cause a lot of problems if contested."

Joyce Holloway fell into a coughing fit, her face reddening. Someone handed her a bottled water, and she chugged.

Dr. Mercer crossed her arms, one perfect eyebrow cocked to the sky.

Ralph looked between us, something dawning slowly.

And the Halford siblings, for the first time, didn't look entirely in control.

Harlan's voice cut clean through it.

"We're going to review the boundaries and make things right. Virginia Marks herself instructed me to do so via documentation she kept in a safe deposit box."

"You've found the painting, then?" Lauren asked, her hand brushing her throat.

"It's not just about the painting," he said. "It's about what the painting confirms. What the old maps confirm." He paused. "If there's one thing I've learned as a lawman, the truth doesn't stay buried forever."

Then he turned slightly, his eyes landing on one person.

Joyce Holloway.

# Chapter Twenty-Eight

"Ms. Holloway," Harlan said gently. "Do you have something to add?"

She blinked rapidly, like she hadn't expected to be called into the light. "Well, um, no?"

"You've been awfully quiet," he said. "Given all this concerns your family's land too."

Another flicker of something—what? Guilt? Nervousness?

I knew I'd be nervous as a cat in a rocking chair factory if I'd been called out like that. But it had to be done.

Her expression changed quickly, from dismay to displeasure. "I am utterly and thoroughly insulted, Sheriff Brooks, if you're implying . . ."

He stopped her. "Not implying anything. Just wondering if you had anything to add to this discussion."

And then it hit me like a . . . brick. "You recognized it," I said.

"I'm sorry?" she said.

"You recognized the name," I said. "When I said the Benino parcel."

"I don't believe I—"

"You didn't look confused," I said. "There was a flicker of recognition."

Delaney stepped in, smooth as ever. "I think we're drifting into speculation again—"

"No," Harlan said. Not quite a bark but it had some bite.

And just like that, Delaney stopped talking.

Joyce rubbed her forehead so hard I thought she might break skin. "I've lived here my entire life," she said. "I've seen many names. And honestly, I don't recall a Benino parcel of land. But the whole discussion just got me wondering. There could be some lines that shouldn't have been drawn. Or were misdrawn. Or redrawn. Whatever. I'm not going to stand here and pretend like that isn't possible."

"Are you a part of the developmental project?" I asked. Harlan probably knew every name, but he hadn't shared it with me.

Joyce drew back her chin and frowned. "Absolutely not. I'm highly against it, in fact."

Dr. Mercer spoke. "I've seen it too. I—" She stopped herself, as if suddenly aware she was stepping into deeper water than she'd intended.

Every head turned toward her.

"Please continue, Dr. Mercer," Harlan said.

She tapped her pen against the legal pad. "I'd never had the chance to meet with Virginia, but in preparation for our first meeting about the painting's value and provenance, I did some research. I know how history can get skewed over time; this is part of what I do. I had already been reviewing the area because I planned to invest in the spa development on the Halford land. And I did become an investor. I am."

She paused, biting her upper lip, then continued. "But I did see earlier references to the land, including the name *Benino*—though I promise I never put two and two together when I met you, Betty. At the time, it seemed like just another old family reference buried in incomplete records. I presumed the property had been sold or otherwise transferred over time.

Plenty of that happens without proper documentation, not just here but many places."

"Those property lines are accurate," Lauren said with some steel behind her words. "They belong exactly where they are, and I will not have a quibble from undocumented history get in the way of our development project, which has many investors, and will only enhance the attractiveness of Bluejay Ridge for tourists and residents alike." She sucked in a breath, then closed her mouth. As if she'd said too much.

A murmur moved through the room at that—part disbelief, part offense.

Beau shifted beside Delaney, who dropped his gaze to study his shiny shoes.

"But it does matter, Lauren," Harlan said.

Delaney stepped forward. "I think we're done here—"

"No," Harlan said. "We're just getting started."

"You're making a mistake," Joyce cut in, and heads swiveled in her direction.

"Then help us out," Harlan replied. "Explain what you mean."

"It was never meant to be separate."

"Meaning?"

Joyce's gaze flicked toward the Halford siblings, and it was a snarl. Lauren Halford snarled back.

This was getting better every minute.

"It was absorbed," Joyce said. "Years ago."

Dr. Mercer scoffed, "Absorbed into what?"

Joyce didn't look at her.

"Into the larger Halford property," she said. "Before your current records. Before any of this became . . . relevant again."

"And the painting?" I asked.

"My grandfather painted that landscape, the trio, to reflect the land before it had been . . . corrected."

"The stone wall."

She nodded.

A ripple went through the room again. People shifted, whispered, looked from the maps to the Joyce Holloway to the Halford siblings as if everyone had been standing on a floorboard that had suddenly gone soft beneath their feet.

Lauren Halford threw her arms up. "It's a painting, for chrissakes. It isn't meant to be literal."

"Oh but it was," Joyce said. "That's the only way my granddaddy painted."

That was the moment I stopped looking at Joyce and started looking harder at not Lauren, but Beau. Joyce looked angry, put-upon, even a little guilty for what she had kept to herself. Lauren was agitated and maybe even frazzled. Beau looked like none of those things. He had been calm, but now he looked like a cornered animal. Like every word about old lines and corrected land struck him somewhere personal.

"You . . ." Beau moved toward Joyce, speaking through gritted teeth. "You donated those other two paintings to start a fuss." He fisted his hands as he approached her, and Ralph bravely yanked him to the side, reprimanding him.

"You did it to suss out the other painting, didn't you?" Lauren finished for her brother. "To question the boundaries. Because you don't want our spa! How could you, Joyce?"

"Please. It's not like we're family friends," Joyce said flatly.

No one in the room looked shocked by her words.

They were just plain ol' fact.

# Chapter Twenty-Nine

By the time I found it, I'd almost walked right past it.

Which, I supposed, was exactly why it had lasted this long.

The road narrowed to little more than a tight hiking path, dipping into a stretch of woods.

I parked beside a leaning fence post—no wire, no signage, just the ghost of something that used to divide one thing from another—and stepped out into the quiet.

No reason, at first glance, to believe this wild land belonged to anyone other than the Halfords, whose property stretched around and beyond it, acres upon acres.

"Hello, family," I whispered.

I moved carefully through the trees, pushing past a tangle of brush, my old sneakers catching on roots and vines and briars and burrs. Hardly dressed for the occasion, but it was all I had in my truck. And there was no delaying when family secrets were waiting to be told.

And then I saw it.

A low stretch of stone masonry, half-swallowed by moss and time. And just beyond it, a narrow chimney stack, broken at the top, darkened with use and age. I approached with reverence, a new connection to my Salvy.

"Here it is, darling. You didn't even know," I spoke to him like I always did, as if he were still right there beside me. In the flesh. "Or maybe you did know and didn't think it mattered much." I stood atop the stone wall. "But it sure does."

The place felt magical. Not pretty, or well-tended, or like anything in a brochure. Just old and wild and free. Honest. Eternal.

But I wasn't only here to confirm the land's whereabouts and gaze upon some Benino history. I was here for another reason, one that had been tapping at the inside of my skull ever since Harlan and I had met in his office, looking over Virginia's notes.

I leaned over to push aside some brush with my gloved hands. Then I moved to look inside the chimney, steadying myself on the ragged edges. "Now, where are you?" I murmured.

A sound came from somewhere behind me.

"I'm right here, Benino."

I whirled around, losing my balance and nearly toppling to my knees next to the chimney. I caught myself and glared at the interloper coming through the trees.

In one hand, he held a pistol loosely at his side.

Hunting?

For what?

Or whom?

Anger rose within me. I would defend this place with my heart and soul. "Beau Halford, get off my land."

He stepped closer, posture relaxed in contradiction to the wicked sneer on his face. My eyes landed on his work boots.

*Looks like a size ten to me.*

"I was hoping you wouldn't come out here," he said. "Though I suppose I should've known you would. You've got that look about you."

"You killed Virginia," I said, wanting to hear him admit it, even though there were no witnesses. "Your little project mattered more than a human being."

He gave a short laugh, but there was nothing funny in it. "You think this is about one little project?" He shrugged. "Maybe the spa won't push through anymore. Or maybe it will. But I have a big problem with anyone who snoops in my family business."

He took another step, the pistol still low but no less real for it.

"I come from a long line of fighters, Benino. Warriors. It's who we are."

"You're a load of baloney," I said, though my voice shook. "Put that thing down before you hurt someone else."

He tilted his head, almost studying me. "You know, you're a smart one. You figured it out faster than I expected. I thought I might make it here first."

"Well, you didn't. And you're trespassing. You need to go."

Beau smiled then, but it was thin and mean. "No, you do."

He lifted the gun—not all the way, not yet, but enough to make me twitch.

I swallowed, willing my breath to steady. "What happened with Virginia, Beau?"

His jaw flexed.

"Did you hunt her down in her own yard?" I asked. "Did you confront her over the painting? Over the land?"

He didn't answer.

He didn't have to.

"You knew she had figured something out. Something big," I said. "You knew the painting wasn't just a painting. You knew it could blow up your spa plans and every pretty promise made to investors. So you went after her."

"She was stubborn," he snapped. "I couldn't have that."

There it was.

Not a confession. Not yet. But close enough to smell the stink.

"She wouldn't stop," he went on. "She thought because she had one old painting and a handful of scraps, she got to decide what happened to all of us. To this town. To land claims that had been settled generations ago."

"Settled," I said. "Or stolen?"

His face hardened. "Watch yourself."

"No," I said, surprising myself with how steady I sounded. "You watch yourself. This was never yours."

For one brief second, something passed over his face—anger, yes, but underneath it something more ragged. Fear, maybe. Or the dawning realization that the thing he'd tried to stomp flat had come back to life with a vengeance.

"She slipped," he said.

I stared at him.

"That's what you're going with?"

He exhaled hard through his nose. "I went there to talk sense into her. That's all. She got worked up. She started in on me about surveys and records and what my family had no right to touch. She wouldn't hand over the painting, wouldn't tell me where it was. She turned, lost her footing—"

"No." The word came out flat and cold.

He blinked. "Yes."

"And what? She lost her footing and happened to fall back into the knife you were holding? Oh, please. That's not what happened. Because if it had been an accident, you wouldn't have broken into her house. You wouldn't have thrown a brick at me. You wouldn't have written *Beninos* on it like some backwoods threat. You wouldn't be standing here with a gun."

He had no immediate response. His expression went blank, like he'd forgotten what we were talking about.

Then he began to laugh. He laughed until he cried.

His fingers tightened around the pistol. "You don't know what pressure does to a man."

"I know what cowardice looks like."

His nostrils flared. "I'm getting bored with this conversation." He looked away for half a second, toward the chimney, toward the trees, anywhere but at me. "She should have minded her own business. If she had, I wouldn't have had to—"

"Prey on her? Stab her? Kill her?" I finished for him.

"Yes," he hissed. "And I'd do it again."

There it was. And it was enough. Beau Halford had murdered Virginia in cold blood, the equivalent of shooting her in the back, only with a knife. He didn't register an ounce of regret.

My only regret was that no one but me had heard it.

"All of this," I said, gesturing to the stones, the chimney, the strip of forgotten land, "over a line no one could even see anymore."

"It mattered," he said.

"Not that much."

His gaze flicked back to mine, and this time there was no swagger in it. Just anger and panic all tangled together.

He raised the gun fully. "Maybe not to you."

A crack of fear shot through me, clean and bright. My body went cold even as my mind raced. There was nowhere to run without turning my back on him, which had been proven to be a bad idea. And there was no point in begging a man who'd already decided everyone else's life was negotiable.

So I held my ground.

"You shoot me," I said, "and this whole mountain is going to come down on you."

"Maybe," he said. "Maybe I'm tired of people underestimating what I'm willing to do for family."

A sound stirred in the trees to my left. Small. Easy to miss. Beau's eyes shifted just slightly in that direction. Mine did not. No way I was taking my eyes off that pistol.

"Hold." The clicking of weaponry echoed through our space. "You're done here, Halford."

And out of the trees stepped two men, well known to me and this town. My heroes. The sheriff holding a rifle and sweet Uncle Earl looking properly irritated. Relief swelled through me.

But Beau wasn't done.

He ran.

Uncle Earl took the shot.

With a rock the size of Trudy's hand, Uncle Earl clocked that cream puff hard on the head, sending him straight to the ground, his gun flying off into the tall grass somewhere beyond.

The whole thing happened so fast my brain barely kept up with it—one second Beau was lunging for freedom, the next he was cursing and clawing at the dirt.

As Beau howled and rolled, Uncle Earl removed some rope from his pocket and headed that way. Harlan approached me. "Blast it, Betty. You okay?"

"Whoa." I blew out a long breath. "Yes. Everything's going to be okay, and Virginia's murder won't be in vain."

My knees picked then to remember themselves, and I wobbled. Near death experiences had a way of doing that to a person. I locked my knees and managed to stay upright.

"Oh!" I said, holding up a finger. I remembered the whole reason I'd come here. I scurried over to the chimney, peered inside, then dug my hand around. Beau could be heard in the background, shouting, and explaining, and defending himself.

And then, over Earl's low growl and Harlan's sharper orders, Beau spilled it—about Virginia, about the mountain properties, about shutting her up for good. Whatever scraps of doubt or word-twisting that remained blew away like ash.

A knife in the back, just like the coward he was.

With great care, I pulled what I presumed was the painting out of its hiding spot. I unwrapped the sheets that covered it, and my instincts were confirmed.

"I present to you the missing Holloway."

# Chapter Thirty

"Let's get that beauty down to the historical society," Harlan said. "Good work, Betty. Though next time, maybe mention your plan before you go wandering into the woods. Darn near got yourself killed."

We strode side by side through the tall grass and toward his Bronco. Uncle Earl was corralling Beau in the same direction behind us.

"It's like we're partners," I said, grinning stupidly. "Starsky and Hutch."

"Hardly."

"We've solved two murders together, you and me."

"Hardly." But there was less resistance in it this time. He chuckled.

"You're a lot like your Uncle Earl, you know," I told him, grabbing his arm to steady myself over a pile of rocks. "A man of few words, but with his eye on the ball."

"That's a huge compliment, Betty Benino. You're not so bad yourself."

I looked over at him then—really looked. At the set of his shoulders, the calm in him even after all that, the way he moved through the aftermath like a man comfortable with carrying heavy things without dropping them. Harlan Brooks was not flashy. He wasn't warm and fuzzy either. And he certainly wasn't chatty. But he was steady and reliable and fair. And on this day in particular, when I'd nearly been killed by a very bad man, those qualities meant everything.

"You got there fast," I said.

He glanced at me. "You think I was going to let you have all the fun?"

I laughed, and something in my chest loosened.

No more was said for a bit. We just walked, one foot in front of the other . . . through the grass, through the fading light, past one old line after another. But something had changed between us. Less like a sheriff keeping an eye on a troublesome old woman, and more like mutual respect.

# Chapter Thirty-One

The Bluejay Ridge Historical Society had never looked better. And renovations had not even begun yet. The fundraiser, however, would make sure it all happened and then some.

String lights had been draped along the beams of the main hall, softening the angles of the old building and casting everything in a warm glow. Along the walls were tables laden with auction items, townsfolk clamoring to get in a bid. And center stage at the back of the room, the Winter Garden series in all its glory—displayed in memory of Virginia Marks and her fight for the preservation of this town's history. I'd personally crafted the wording on the plaques with care.

Food trucks were parked outside, and the yummy smells wafted throughout the space through the open front doors.

I stood just inside the doorway for a moment, taking it in.

People laughed. Champagne glasses clinked. Someone had brought a fiddle, and a low, easy melody threaded its way through the hum of conversation.

If you didn't know better, you'd think this was just another small-town gathering—one more excuse to eat too much, overspend on silent-auction items, and pretend nobody had recently unearthed a murder, a land dispute, and a family scandal all at once.

"Don't just stand there," Maybelline called from across the room.

“What would you have me do now?” I shot back. “I haven’t done enough?”

She nudged me with a snicker. “Dance, Betty Benino. Dance with me.”

And to my surprise, she joined her elbow with mine and dragged me deeper into the room. We twirled and twirled, and I laughed hysterically. Others soon joined in.

“Is this a hoedown?” I shouted.

“Of course it is!”

I saw Trudy and Jolene walk inside, and I urged them over. They didn’t hesitate.

Trudy’s cane led the way, and they danced side by side, a slight swaying of the hips. Jolene putting a little more effort into it, along with raised arms. “Woo-hoo,” she sang.

Maybelline laughed. There was a bright pink in her cheeks and delight in her eyes. She was in her element. And truth be told, so was I.

“I told you we’d pull it off,” she said as she spun past me. “People like a good comeback.”

Ralph Jenkins stood near the center table, one hand resting lightly on the back of a chair, as if it might wander off if he didn’t keep an eye on it. His smile was wide, something I hadn’t seen in a long time.

He caught my eye and gave a small nod.

I bowed in his direction, drawing my colorful tiered skirt out to the side. Trudy poked me in the backside with her cane, and I whipped around to shoot a teasing glare at her. Her shoulders bounced as she laughed, then she two-stepped her way to the other side of the room.

A couple more fiddle players and one guitarist joined in

for a fresh song, and I stepped out of the fray. Glancing at the paintings, I noticed . . .

There was an extra plaque in the middle. What in the world?

Dodging a few visitors, I rushed in that direction and . . . gasped.

A new plaque. One I hadn't written or even seen before.

It was about Antonio Benino and his family, how they had unwittingly played a part in a town mystery that would be talked about for ages.

I teared up, turning to find Maybelline approaching, tears also in her eyes.

"It had to be said, Betty."

"Virginia would've liked that."

Joyce Holloway came up behind me with a big hug. "Yes, she would have."

We stood there a moment, looking at the painting. Not speaking.

Around us, people kept moving—laughing, bidding, eating, living. But right there in front of those paintings, time seemed to hold still for just a beat.

Because art didn't require words. Just heart.

And Bluejay Ridge had plenty of it.

# Chapter Thirty-Two

Two trucks were parked at the curb in front of the cottage. I'd nearly forgotten I'd signed the contract weeks ago, right before all the fundraising business had swallowed my calendar. I was in the process of unloading more garden goodies from my Jeep. And yes, plenty of groceries too. A girl had to eat.

The old fencing had already been taken down by the time I got home.

It had been serviceable. Tall wooden slats, weathered gray, practical in a keep-the-dog-in, keep-the-world-out sort of way. But it had always blocked the view. You had to be up on my patio, at the top of the slope to my backyard, to see the shimmer of Lake Bluejay through the trees. I wanted more.

So I ordered wrought iron instead. Strong, open lines. Something I could see through.

The contractors worked quickly as I busied myself in the house. By dusk, it was finished. Black wrought iron with simple vertical bars and a gentle arch at the top. The spires were pineapples.

Delightful in every possible way. I paid the bill and tipped them generously.

Now, seated inside the gazebo, where I'd placed fresh cushions around the benches, I could see it.

The whole wide blue stretch of the lake, catching the remnants of daylight like a big gemstone.

"Goodness gracious," Trudy said, lowering herself into

one of the wicker chairs I'd placed in the center of the gazebo, facing out toward the lake. "Why in the world did you wait this long?"

"No idea."

"I absolutely love it. We'll have to visit more often," Jolene said.

I put my hands in a prayer position and looked to the sky. "Help me, Lord."

We'd gathered there with plates of chicken salad and a pitcher of sweet tea—with a smidge of Honey Jack Daniel's, of course.

The air held that early spring softness that North Georgia so generously gives its people. Just enough warmth to convince your shoulders to drop . . . and to dream.

Harlan stood near the new fence, hands on his hips.

He did not sit.

"This is a terrible idea," he said.

I smiled at his back. "It's beautiful."

"It's transparent."

"That's the point."

"Anyone can walk right up."

"Anyone could walk right up before," I reminded him. "They just couldn't see the lake while they did it."

He turned slowly, giving me that look he reserved for my more impractical declarations.

"Electric fence," he muttered. "That's what you need."

Trudy perked up. "Now that would be something."

"Let's not get crazy," Jolene said. "I don't think ol' Nutty would appreciate that much."

I toasted to that comment. "Nutty would fry."

As if summoned, the squirrel bounded along the edge of

the yard, tail high, pausing to inspect one of the iron posts.

"He'll adjust," I said.

Harlan walked the length of the fence once more, testing the gate latch. "You should add a padlock, at least."

As if an intruder couldn't just hop right over the thing.

"You're certain you feel safe?" he asked finally.

I looked past him to the lake.

The trees were just beginning to bud. Not full leaves yet—just that faint haze of green that meant the world was waking up. My snowdrops, stubborn and delicate, nodded along the edge of the garden bed. I'd left them in place, of course. They were winter's quiet survivors. Like many of us.

"I do," I said. And I meant it.

Lauren Halford, having had no idea what her brother had done, withdrew the spa proposal publicly the morning after her brother's arraignment. She'd cited "community concerns and historical ambiguities." Dr. Mercer had spoken publicly about respecting due process and preserving Bluejay Ridge's heritage. Ralph had delivered a speech at the fundraiser about transparency, though he perspired heavily throughout the whole affair.

Bless his heart.

The paintings remained on display at the historical society. And plans for upgrading the building were making fast headway, now that we had the money tucked away to fund it all.

Harlan finally sat down, though he positioned his chair so he could see both the lake and the driveway.

"You're not installing cameras?" he asked.

"I might," I said. "But not because I'm afraid."

He studied me.

"And why then?"

"I want to see the animals come to the lake." I gazed in that direction, remembering the deer I had seen plenty of times. And even one brown bear.

That earned the smallest ghost of a smile. "A very good reason," he admitted, then got up to pour himself another liquor-laced glass of tea.

The lake shifted colors as the sun dropped lower. A pontoon boat drifted lazily near the far bank. Somewhere across the water, a dog barked, answered by another farther down.

I thought of the North Georgia Beninos and their land with pride. Salvy would have loved it. The kids . . . yeah, we were going to have some fun thinking about what we might want to do with it—if it belonged to us at all. It might turn out to be another branch of the Benino tree entirely. Something we'd figure out eventually.

That was a history assignment I could really sink my teeth into.

"This where the party's at?" a voice bellowed.

"Come on in, Hank," I said, waving him through the gate. "Let me get you set up."

He whistled as he gazed around the backyard and beyond. "Now this is something. I'm going to have to do the same."

"But you don't have a big fence up," I said.

"Right. But this looks really cool. I need a new handyman project."

"Well, Betty," Harlan said, "if you insist on leaving your yard open to the world, at least let me buy you better outdoor lighting."

Trudy clapped her thigh and hooted. "Now we're talking."

I beamed. "I'll allow it. But I'll pay for it. You install it?"

"I can do that."

Lighting was something I had absolutely planned to do anyway. But Harlan's input was a pleasant surprise.

Hank raised his hand. "I'll help."

I chuckled. *Of course he will, that devil.*

The sun slipped lower, leaving the lake in soft lavender shadow. The wrought iron fence cast thin lines across the yard, and I admired the symmetry for a moment. The yard was really coming into its own.

And sitting there in my little patch of Lake Pointe, with my snowdrops nodding and my view wide open at last, I felt something settle deep in my chest.

Gratitude to Ms. Virginia Marks.

The lines had held.

And so would I.

[illegible] absolutely pleased to do [illegible]

[illegible] Hungary [illegible] pleasant [illegible]

[illegible] help."

[illegible] Of course [illegible] not dead."

[illegible]

[illegible]

[illegible]

[illegible]

And sitting here on my little patch of [illegible], with my snowdrops nodding and my [illegible] wide open at last, I felt something settle deep in my chest.

[illegible]

The [illegible] End.

[illegible]

# Join the Friends of Frenzy

Betty has become so beloved that we're celebrating the release of *Secrets in the Snowdrops* with a little something special—a commemorative pin for her biggest fans, a.k.a. the Friends of Frenzy.

Want in? Visit my website at www.janetfix.com, join the newsletter, and send me a quick email to let me know you've picked up one of Betty's books: janet@janetfix.com. (An order number, screenshot, or—my favorite—a photo of you holding your copy will do just fine!)

There are more goodies ahead for Betty's Friends of Frenzy, so stay tuned.

In the meantime, I'm already outlining Book 4, *Gossip in the Gardenias,* with plans for a June release—so you won't have to wait long for your next Betty fix.

If you're new to the series or want to share it with a friend, *Mayhem in the Mulch* is where it all begins. The books can be read in any order, but if you like a little method to Betty's madness, it's a good place to start.

And if you've enjoyed spending time with Betty and the crew, a quick review at your favorite retailer helps other readers discover the series—and it means the world to me.

See you soon, fellow Friends of Frenzy.

*— Janet*

# Books by Janet Fix

**BETTY BENINO MYSTERIES**

*Mayhem in the Mulch,* book 1
*Mischief and Mistletoe,* book 2 (a holiday novella)
*Secrets in the Snowdrops,* book 3

***THE SHIPS WE SAIL***: *Modern Fables for the Unfinished Soul*

**SLOANE AND MADDIE, PERIL AWAITS**
**(coauthored with Cheryl Bradshaw)**

*The Silent Boy,* book 1
*The Shadow Children,* book 2
*The Broken Soul,* book 3
*The Widow Maker,* book 4
*The Familiar Stranger,* book 5

**RANCH HERO TRILOGY**
**(children's books)**

*Ranch Hero*
*Ranch Hero 2: Moooving Velma*
*Ranch Hero 3: An Australian Beach Vacation*

And last but not least . . . the **NO WAY!** series for our smallest readers is coming soon, and I can't wait to share it. I'll be releasing the first three books together to kick things off.

# About the Author

Janet Fix is a book publisher, editor, and multi-genre writer whose work spans gripping mysteries, heartwarming children's stories, and soulful modern fables. With decades of publishing experience and global collaborations, Janet balances coaching other authors with her own creative writing.

Outside the world of books, Janet is a passionate researcher, avid gardener, and devoted grandmother to four granddaughters. She finds joy in the exploration of words, the quiet power of manifestation, and the healing energy of nature and intention—helping others find the courage to tell their own stories.

Learn more and join her newsletter at **www.janetfix.com**